OUTNUMBERED!

Longarm said loudly, "You're under arrest. Hands up."

The gunman farthest from the door glanced up. Instinctively, his hand went to his revolver and he started to draw. Longarm shot him square in the upper chest, the bullet appearing to drive him downward before it knocked him flat over on his back.

The second gunman was just a half second behind his companion . . .

DON'T MISS THESE
ALL-ACTION WESTERN SERIES
FROM THE BERKLEY PUBLISHING GROUP

THE GUNSMITH by J. R. Roberts
Clint Adams was a legend among lawmen, outlaws, and ladies. They called him . . . the Gunsmith.

LONGARM by Tabor Evans
The popular long-running series about U.S. Deputy Marshal Long—his life, his loves, his fight for justice.

SLOCUM by Jake Logan
Today's longest-running action Western. John Slocum rides a deadly trail of hot blood and cold steel.

TABOR EVANS

LONGARM

AND THE
HOSTAGE WOMAN

JOVE BOOKS, NEW YORK

LONGARM AND THE HOSTAGE WOMAN

A Jove Book / published by arrangement with
the author

PRINTING HISTORY
Jove edition / November 1996

The Putnam Berkley World Wide Web site address is
http://www.berkley.com/berkley

ISBN: 0-515-11968-7

A JOVE BOOK®
Jove Books are published by The Berkley Publishing Group,
200 Madison Avenue, New York, New York 10016.
JOVE and the "J" design are trademarks
belonging to Jove Publications, Inc.

PRINTED IN THE UNITED STATES OF AMERICA

10 9 8 7 6 5 4 3 2 1

Chapter 1

Longarm sat in a saloon in Laredo, Texas, having a drink of whiskey before he went to his hotel room and fell into bed. It was only mid-afternoon but he was bone-weary and sleepless from a harrowing three-day trip from Mexico City with a prisoner. He'd been sent to the Mexican capital to fetch back a man who was accused of having embezzled nearly two hundred thousand dollars from the Federal Reserve banking system. The man had been a well-placed employee in the Treasury Department and he'd simply seen his chance and grabbed money meant for a federal bank in San Antonio. Then he had fled to Mexico, never expecting to be caught. But he had been, and he was being held in a jail in Mexico City while the United States government got the Mexican government to agree to extradite the man. Longarm, to his disgust, had drawn the assignment of fetching back a crook that he deemed no more than a bank clerk. It had meant a hell of a lot of train riding and spending more time in Mexico City than Longarm had cared for, but that hadn't been the

1

rough part that had led to all the loss of sleep. The prisoner had been hard to handle and Longarm had had to resort to force and handcuffs and wrist irons on several occasions. The worst of it had been the warnings, by Mexican officials and by telegraph from the marshal's service, that Longarm should expect an attempt or attempts, at any time, by interested parties to free the man. The money had not been recovered and it had been pointed out, by those who knew, that a man with $200,000 hidden somewhere in Mexico would have a lot of friends.

So it had been three days of virtual sleeplessness. Longarm knew that he could have stayed in Mexico City and waited for another officer to assist him, but he'd decided he'd had enough of the place and was ready to get his prisoner across the border and head himself back to his home base in Denver.

It had been less than an hour since he'd turned the prisoner over to four Texas lawmen who would transfer him on to San Antonio to jail and then to a federal court. Longarm had never been so glad to see the back of a man in all his life. He'd gotten a receipt, headed for the nearest hotel, gotten a room, and then had stepped into the nearest bar to wash a little of the railroad dust out of his throat before he lay down to sleep the clock around.

The prisoner, Earl oCombs, might have been a glorified bank clerk but he hadn't looked or acted much like one. He'd been as much trouble as he could manage to be. Even in shackles he'd tried to give Longarm difficulty until the United States deputy marshal had been forced to let the man understand how painful the barrel of a revolver could feel on the side of the head. Combs was a burly man in his mid-thirties, gone to fat a little, but otherwise strong and hard and determined not to go back to the United States. Longarm had commandeered the conductor's compartment for the trip, figuring it would be best to keep Combs out of the sight of the other passengers and the other passengers out of the sight of Combs. As it was, Combs had to be pulled and jerked onto the train while he loudly and repeatedly offered ten thousand dollars to anyone who would help him escape. It had helped that the man didn't speak Spanish.

Longarm sat tiredly at the table and shook his head, remembering the ordeal. He'd come into the saloon only to buy a bottle to take back to the hotel with him, but then he'd decided he was too tired and too het up to sleep. He'd thought to have one drink in the roomy confines of the saloon—roomy after three days in the small compartment on the train—but now he decided to have another. He could feel the first one starting to unwind him and he figured he'd give it an extra push.

He knew why he'd drawn the damnable assignment. It was his boss's idea of a good joke. Billy Vail, who looked like someone's sainted old grandfather, was, Longarm decided, about the meanest bastard ever to put on a badge and call himself the chief marshal for any territory served by the marshal's service. It had been Longarm's bad luck to have just finished a long hunt for a train robber in the New Mexico Territory. He'd come back to headquarters figuring he deserved a nice long rest and frequent visits to a lady friend who was a dressmaker. But if there was anything that Billy Vail couldn't stand it was to see Longarm at peace and making a good job of fun and relaxation. And then it had been another case of bad luck that Longarm had been in Billy Vail's office when the request for a deputy to go to Mexico City to extradite Combs had come in. It had tickled Billy's sense of whimsy to talk, for about half an hour, about what good times he'd had in the Mexican capital in the past. When Longarm, out of good manners, had carelessly begun to agree

3

with him that, yes, it was a hell of a place, Billy had jumped him with the offer of a quick trip.

Longarm looked sourly into his glass, thinking dire thoughts of how he was going to get back at the old goat. He'd think of something. Naturally, Billy had meant to send him from the moment the request had come in, but he couldn't just out and out tell Longarm. No, he had to build it up and make it sound like some sort of damn vacation. And then, if that wasn't enough, when Longarm protested, Billy had said that Longarm had to go. It wasn't a job he could entrust to just anyone. When Longarm had pointed out that since it was a Treasury crime, it was more a job for a marshal nearer to the border, he'd said, "Ought to be somebody out of the southeast district at the very least."

But Billy Vail, who Longarm knew had already volunteered his services and probably already knew what a bitch of a task it would be, had tried to look shocked.

"This is a Mexican and a border job, Custis, and there's nobody who knows that country better than you. Hell, I'd hate to think how many horses you've bought in Mexico and then shipped back at government expense and sold them off for a profit. Why, a man with that kind of experience can damn near think like an embezzler."

Longarm had given him a sour look and said, "Billy Vail, you are a blackmailing old son of a bitch and you ought to be ashamed of yourself complaining about a poorly paid public servant for trying to help himself out now and again. Hell, if I had a dime for every dollar you've knocked off my expense vouchers I could retire tomorrow."

But there was one thing to be said for arguing with Billy Vail—you weren't going to win. He was the boss and he had the years of experience and the scars to prove it. They were good friends except when it came to poker and handing out assignments. Longarm usually got the best of it in the one and the wrong end of the stick in the other.

Now he sagged down at his table and worked on his second drink. He'd left for Mexico City weighing a little over one hundred and ninety-five pounds and standing an inch or two over six feet. The better part of it had been muscle. Now he felt so drawn and gaunt that he didn't reckon he could stand examination. He figured he had lost ten pounds on the trip and maybe six inches in height. When Combs had seen he was not going to be able to physically escape from Longarm, he had settled into a steady tirade of taunts and abuse and threats. According to Combs, his "friends" would be holding the train up at any mile marker to take him off and make short work of Longarm. Combs had assured the deputy marshal that he would never see the end of the line alive if he didn't let him, Combs, loose.

And when he wasn't threatening he was trying to bribe. At one point, he'd offered Longarm half the missing money and his pick of a whorehouse Combs claimed he owned in New Orleans and that he said housed the best-looking collection of women in the world. Longarm doubted the whorehouse and doubted the women, but he didn't doubt that Combs was the most trouble of any prisoner he had ever handled. As a consequence, he never had a drink in peace, a meal in peace, and certainly no peaceful rest the whole trip.

For some time Longarm had been aware of a man at the bar who kept darting little quick glances his way. The bar was only a couple of yards from his table and the saloon was nearly empty so Longarm had slight doubt that the man was looking at him. He thought it might have something to do with his being a United States deputy marshal, but, as was his custom when he didn't officially need to wear it, his badge was buttoned inside his shirt pocket. Without seeming to, Longarm gave the man a careful examination. There was

5

nothing outstanding about him. He looked like a merchant or a drummer or even maybe a bank clerk of some kind. Longarm guessed him to be closing on forty years of age. The man was of medium size and was wearing a frock coat with a vest and a string tie. He had on a derby hat and was shod in high-top shoes with patent-leather toes. He appeared to be drinking whiskey with a beer chaser. As best as Longarm could see, the man did not appear to be carrying a weapon, but he had made it a habit to always assume that an apparently unarmed man was sure to be carrying a hidden gun somewhere about his person. In his line of work you didn't take anything for granted, not if you expected to continue in that line of work for any length of time. And he had, he thought, continued in the line of work longer than anyone with any sense would have done. His body said thirty, but his work- and weather-wearied face said closer to forty. His name was Custis Long officially, but he was known, on both sides of the law, by the name he'd been given when he'd pursued an outlaw over a thousand miles to bring him back to justice: Longarm. He was the "Long Arm of the Law." It was said that you could run as far as you wanted and dig yourself a hole nearly to China, but just about the time you started getting comfortable, you'd look up and there would be Custis Long standing with his long arm stretched out to drag you back. The general opinion was that Billy Vail had given him the name, but Longarm wasn't so sure about that. One thing he was sure about, however, was that Billy never failed to use it when it suited his purposes, like the Mexico City trip for instance.

He'd said, looking as innocent as the rogue he was, "Why, them folks up in Washington, D.C., asked for you special. They done heard all about the famous Longarm and said it wouldn't do for nobody else to go up and fetch that thief back except for the famous Longarm. No, sir. They won't

6

hear of nobody else doing it.'' Then he'd sighed. ''Price of fame, I'd reckon.''

Billy, Longarm thought, was a handy man with salt if there were any wounds needing treatment.

Longarm caught movement out of the corner of his eye. The man at the bar had turned to give him another looking-over. This time Longarm openly stared back. He couldn't figure the man out. He looked too prosperous to be bumming a drink, but yet he didn't look flashy enough to be some tinhorn gambler thinking maybe he could lure a weary trail-worn cowpoke into a card game. Longarm could not quite make out what the man's business was.

The look Longarm had returned seemed to have beckoned as an invitation to the man. He turned from the bar with a glass in one hand and a whiskey bottle in the other and crossed over the few feet to Longarm's table. He stood there, a moderately sized man, looking down at Longarm. He asked, ''Mind if I sit a spell, neighbor?''

Longarm shoved a chair out with his boot. He was curious about the man if nothing else. ''Why not? Take a chair,'' he said.

The man sat down, looking as innocent and nondescript as he had when Longarm had first laid eyes on him. Now the man offered the bottle across the table.

''Fill that drink up for you?'' he asked.

Longarm gave his half-filled glass a slight nudge forward. He said, ''Why not? Somewhere I heard it never hurts to drink another man's whiskey.''

The stranger said, ''I may go to hell for lying, but I damn sure ain't ever going to hell for turning down a drink.''

Longarm lifted his glass in a toast. He said, ''I'll drink to that.''

They both took a long pull at their glasses and then set

them down almost simultaneously. Longarm asked evenly, "What can I do for you?"

The stranger answered, "You certainly appear to be a man who likes to get right down to business."

Longarm said, "Well, you've pretty well eyed me over. I just can't figure out what for. I can tell you in advance that you ain't got nothing to sell that I want to buy, I ain't looking to play no cards. And if there is any other business that you can think of to keep me from a good night's sleep, it would have to be damned exciting."

The stranger laughed slightly. "Well, I don't know how you feel about making money. Some folks find it kind of exciting," he said.

Longarm gave the man a level look. "Making money? How?"

The stranger fluttered his hand slightly. He said, "Oh, nothing too illegal. Matter of fact, I don't reckon that you could call it illegal at all. It's an easy job."

"Doing what?" Longarm asked.

The stranger said, "Shouldn't that be 'Paying how much?' "

Longarm smiled slightly. He said, "All right. Paying how much?"

The stranger leaned forward and adjusted his frock coat. "A hundred dollars. Spot cash. Gold coins. What do you think of that now?"

Longarm half smiled. He was on the point of telling the man that he very often bet that amount of money on a middling hand of poker, but something stayed his speech. He was curious as to what a stranger would be willing to pay a hundred dollars to another stranger to do. It wasn't so much the lawman in him that was curious as it was just a man sitting in a saloon. "A hundred dollars? Is that a fact? Say, that's a pile of money."

The stranger leaned forward eagerly. He said, "Yep, and it's all in gold." With one hand he reached into the pocket of his frock coat and pulled out five twenty-dollar gold pieces. He let them clink down on the table. "Take a look at that. *Oro puro*. Pure gold. Yellow as butter." He pushed two of the coins to one side and pulled three back toward himself. He said, "Forty now and sixty when you do the job."

Longarm looked at him curiously. He asked, "What the hell am I supposed to do? I'm not going to kill anybody if that's what you got in mind."

The stranger laughed. "Oh, nothing quite that extreme. Actually, it's a simple job that shouldn't take you more than maybe three or four hours." He leaned forward again. "I'm sure a man in your position could make good use of a hundred dollars."

Longarm wasn't sure he cared for that kind of talk. True, he must look a little shopworn and hard used after three days on a train with a maniac, but he was still wearing a $40 hat and an $80 pair of boots and a $100 concave silver buckle on his belt that usually concealed a .38-caliber derringer in its concave shape.

He asked, "You mean, you're just going to give me forty dollars and let me walk out of here with it?"

The man nodded. "Yep. Just like that."

"What makes you so sure that I'll come back?"

The stranger said, tapping his head, "I'm a man as knows people, neighbor. Name is Jenkins. I make it my business to know what folks will do and you look like a good honest hired hand to me."

Longarm barely controlled a slight twinge of temper. He personally didn't think he looked much like a hired hand and about the only person he allowed to talk to him in such a manner was Billy Vail and the only reason for that was Billy

9

Vail was his boss. Now here was a complete stranger talking to him as if he was a trail hand, not that he had anything against trail hands. It was just that he would have to be about the oldest one on the trail, with the average age of such cowhands being between nineteen and twenty, and at his age he would have been a failed trail hand.

He looked at the stranger. "Well, Mr. Jenkins. As I understand it, I'm to get forty dollars for going out and doing something and another sixty dollars when I get back. Now, what exactly is it you want me to do?"

Mr. Jenkins looked carefully around, though there wasn't another ear within fifteen feet. Still, he leaned forward and in a hushed voice said, "Well, it's really fairly simple. All I want you to do is go across the border about three or four miles on the other side of Nuevo Laredo where you are going to find a horse. A good-looking, high-blooded Arabian horse. I want you to bring that horse back to me right here in this saloon. That's all there is to it."

Longarm pulled his head back slightly as if he hadn't quite heard. He asked, "You want me to go four miles deep into Mexico and fetch you back a horse?"

"You heard correctly. I didn't quite get your name, by the way."

Longarm said, "You didn't get it because I didn't send it. Name is . . . well, let's just say my name is Jones."

Mr. Jenkins nodded. "Fine with me, Mr. Jones, or whatever you want it to be. That's good enough for me."

Longarm asked, "And when I bring the horse back here to you in the saloon, what then?"

Mr. Jenkins said, "Why, then I give you the other sixty dollars." With his hand, he motioned to the three coins he had pulled toward himself. "Making a round hundred dollars you've earned for about four hours' work. Tell me where you can do better than that?"

"Well, I can't think of any place right off outside of the United States Senate," Longarm said.

Mr. Jenkins chuckled like a man not quite used to laughing. He said, "Oh, that's a good one. Will you do it?"

Longarm rubbed his jaw reflectively. He couldn't quite figure out what Mr. Jenkins's game was but he knew it was crooked because Mr. Jenkins now began to look crooked. He said, "Well, I don't know, Mr. Jenkins. It sounds way too easy. Just going and fetching a horse? A hundred dollars? That must be some horse. You got trouble getting across the border through the custom inspectors? That horse got some kind of quarantine problems?"

"No, no, no," Mr. Jenkins said. He put his hands out. "That horse will have his proper quarantine papers. You'll have no trouble crossing with the horse."

Longarm said, "Well, to begin with, you want me to go four miles across into Mexico. I ain't going to walk and I'm afoot right now."

Mr. Jenkins said, shaking his head, "It doesn't matter. I've got a good saddle horse hitched right outside. You just get on him and you're on your way. Now, what do you say to the deal?"

Longarm didn't know quite what to say. His body was begging him to go to bed, but his mind was intrigued to know what kind of crime Mr. Jenkins was trying to involve him in. He didn't know for certain that Mr. Jenkins had crime in mind, but the idea of paying someone a hundred dollars simply to fetch a horse four miles into Mexico made him stop and ponder. He said, looking at Mr. Jenkins carefully, "Well, sir. That is a mighty interesting proposition. One thing I am curious about. Why don't you go get the horse yourself?"

As he looked down at the gold Mr. Jenkins said, "Well, this right here"—he tapped the gold coins—"is supposed to keep me from having to answer that question, but I don't mind answering it. To tell you the truth, there was bad blood sprung up between me and the man that I bought that horse from. I don't want no trouble. I'm not a fighting man and I would rather not run into this particular hombre again."

"I see," Longarm said. He looked thoughtfully around the still-deserted saloon. "Still and all, Mr. Jenkins. You'll have to admit that's quite a bit of money for a short job like that. There's twenty vaqueros right out there on the street who would do that job for you for a tenth of the amount you're offering."

Jenkins nodded his head vigorously. He said, "That's true enough, Mr. Jones, but I like the way you look. I like your style. I've got a feeling that I am dealing with an honest cattleman. Now, if I go out there and hire one of those fellows off the street, he's likely to take my ten dollars, go get the horse, take the horse and keep on going. I think that you'll take my forty dollars and come back to collect the sixty dollars and bring me my horse. Now, how does that strike you?"

Longarm half smiled. He said, "Mr. Jenkins, excuse me for thinking this, but it doesn't seem quite the sum of the matter. Is that horse carrying anything, by the way? Anything on his back?"

Mr. Jenkins looked puzzled. He said, "I don't know what you mean."

Longarm asked, "Well, does he have a saddle on?"

"Yes, there's a saddle that goes with him," Mr. Jenkins said, nodding slowly.

"That high-priced horse gets a saddle thrown in with him? A horse that you'd spend a hundred dollars to fetch? Do you mind me asking how much you spent for that animal?"

Mr. Jenkins looked slightly ruffled. "Yes, I do mind you asking me how much I paid for the horse, but as for the

12

saddle, it's a good one and it came with the horse. Why should I turn it down?''

"And does it have a pair of saddlebags on behind the saddle?'' asked Longarm gently.

Mr. Jenkins looked concerned. He said, "Yes, I suppose so. Mr. Jones, I don't quite understand why you are asking all these questions. All I am asking you to do is go get a horse and bring him back. The horse has been paid for, he's not stolen, he's got good quarantine papers on him, and I'm asking you to go and get him because I don't want to run into the hombre that sold him to me. That's all there is to it and you make a hundred dollars. What's the confusion here?''

Longarm leaned lazily back in his chair and stared up at a spot on the ceiling. He picked up his whiskey and lifted the glass to his lips and sipped slowly for a moment. It wasn't good whiskey, neither the bottle he'd bought nor the bottle Mr. Jenkins had brought over. None of it was good whiskey. What he yearned for was a taste of the good Maryland whiskey that he kept a supply of in Denver, but he wouldn't get any more of that until he got back. Now here he was thinking about delaying his trip home out of curiosity about what Mr. Jenkins was up to. Not that he would actually be delaying his trip; he wouldn't be able to get a train until noon the next day. All he would be doing was delaying sleep for about four hours. But he had a strong curiosity, which was a powerful tool for a lawman.

He turned to Mr. Jenkins and said, "Now, Mr. Jenkins. The thought comes to my mind that there might be something in those saddlebags that you wouldn't care for the United States Custom Service to be looking into. Would there be any fact to that business?''

Mr. Jenkins drew himself up straighter. "Why, sir. I resent

that remark. That is a question that no gentleman should ask of another.''

Longarm said gently, ''You forget, Mr. Jenkins, I'm not a gentleman, so I don't know what a gentleman is supposed to ask. I don't want to find out when I get to the border that I am carrying a load of gold or some other contraband that might get me in a world of trouble with the border people. Now if you were sitting in my chair, wouldn't you maybe think that such a thing was possible?''

Mr. Jenkins relaxed somewhat from the formal posture that he had taken. He said, ''Well, yes, I suppose I can see where you might. But I can assure you, sir, that no such thing is intended. There is simply this: a horse has to be brought back. Nothing more, nothing less. You may, if you care to, search the saddle and the saddlebags, and anything that you believe to be contraband, you can cast aside. I simply want the horse back over here on this side of the border.''

Longarm pulled a cigarillo out of his shirt pocket and lit it with a match that he struck with a scratch on his boot heel. He said, ''Well, I've got to tell you, Mr. Jenkins. I'm kind of dead for some sleep. I figure you can find somebody else for this job without too much trouble. I can't have the only honest face in town.''

Mr. Jenkins said, ''Aw, now, sir. Mr. Jones, please don't say that. I really would appreciate it if you would do this favor for me. Matter of fact, I would even up the ante. I'll make it one hundred twenty dollars.''

Longarm looked at him, his curiosity piqued once more. ''You seem to want that horse powerful bad.''

Mr. Jenkins replied earnestly, ''I do, Mr. Jones, and as far as I am concerned, you are the man for this job. Where would I find another honest man in this place? This is a den of thieves, Mr. Jones, and I'm sure you know the border as well as I do. It's a difficult place. I'm a small man, I'm not

14

a fighter, I don't carry a gun. What chance would I have with the ruffians around here?''

Longarm looked at him levelly for a long time. There was something so frantic, so earnest about Mr. Jenkins that Longarm could not suppress the feeling that the man was up to something crooked, although what it was he could not say. There were, in the setup of the scheme, possible avenues for several methods of wrongdoing. For instance, the horse might be stolen. Maybe Longarm was expected to bring back a stolen horse. Well, if that was the case, Mr. Jenkins had definitely picked the wrong man to send for a stolen horse. He would shortly find himself in the jailhouse wishing he had found himself a different trail-worn, dusty cowhand than one who happened to carry a deputy marshal's badge in his pocket. He decided to play Mr. Jenkins a little more.

He said, ''Mr. Jenkins, I can't quite see my way clear to doing that.''

''Mr. Jones, I beg of you, please, sir. I'd like to make my time in this town short. I'll up the ante to one hundred forty dollars. I'll give you sixty dollars now and eighty when you get back. You surely can't turn that down for four hours' work.''

Longarm asked, ''Have you got clear papers on that horse, Mr. Jenkins?''

''Oh, yes, of course, of course. If that is what is making you hesitate, let me assure you, I have clear title to that horse.'' Jenkins reached into the pocket of his coat and brought out two sheets of paper and handed both of them over to Longarm. One was a bill of sale and the other was a letter of quarantine, describing the horse in detail and the brand he wore.

Longarm looked over the papers carefully. They certainly looked authentic enough. He asked, ''And this is the horse that I will find across the border?''

Mr. Jenkins nodded his head up and down and said, "Yes, that is the horse."

Longarm could not fight his curiosity down. He swore softly to himself for being such a damn fool. The four hours that he was going to waste doing this was four hours that he needed for sleep. He didn't want or need $140; though $140 for four hours' work was considerably better than he did in the marshal's office. He slowly folded the papers and put them on the table in front of him. He asked, "What if I do it in the morning, Mr. Jenkins? Will that suit you?"

Jenkins shook his head violently from side to side. "No, sir. I want to be out of this country before nightfall. I'd like to see that horse back over here and me on my way, even before dark. Please, Mr. Jones, I'm begging you."

Longarm sighed. "Oh, what the hell. Mr. Jenkins, I want to tell you, though, that you may be the one who gets a surprise in this deal."

A slight smile pricked at the corners of Mr. Jenkins's mouth. He said, "Oh, I don't know about that, Mr. Jones. Everybody gets a surprise every once in a while."

Longarm looked at the small man. "Yeah, but not quite the way they expect."

Longarm and Mr. Jenkins stood outside on the street in front of the saloon beside an average-looking roan saddle horse. Longarm had looked the animal over and found him to be sound. He wasn't anything he would write home about, but he figured the horse would make it four miles over there and four miles back.

"Now, let me get these directions straight again, Mr. Jenkins. I go through Nuevo Laredo, and once I've gone through good and clear, I ride on for a couple or three miles and I'll see a small white adobe shack with red tile on the roof. Is that right?"

16

Mr. Jenkins nodded again. "Yes, sir. That's the fact of the matter."

"Do you have any idea how many adobe shacks with red tile roofs there are in this part of the country?" asked Longarm.

"But this will be one of the first that you'll see on your way. There are two Mexican fellows holding the horse for me. There is a corral out back with a barn made out of lumber, kind of gray-looking, sitting back off the road a piece."

Longarm asked, "And that's the road to Monterrey, correct?"

"Yes, sir. You've got it right."

Longarm put a foot in the stirrup of the roan and swung easily aboard. The reins were already looped over the saddle horn. He took them in hand as he looked down at Mr. Jenkins. He said, "Well, sir. I hope that I don't have any trouble finding this horse. Do you realize that I am nearly dead for sleep?"

"Mr. Jones, I consider this a mighty fine favor that you are doing me and I certainly will appreciate it," said Mr. Jenkins.

Longarm nodded. He was about to say "So long" when Mr. Jenkins suddenly shoved his hand in his pocket. It came out holding three twenty-dollar gold pieces.

"Mr. Jones, you are about to forget your money."

Longarm looked down at the gold coins in the man's hand. He said, "Well, let's do it this way, Mr. Jenkins. If I get your horse back over here, you can pay me the whole thing at one time." He gave Mr. Jenkins a significant look. "But if I run into trouble I won't feel like I am beholden to you in any way. In other words, I won't be working for you, Mr. Jenkins, until I get back over here with the horse. Do you understand me?"

Mr. Jenkins assumed an innocent look. He said, "Why, I

don't have any idea what you are a-talkin' about, Mr. Jones."

Longarm grinned and reined the horse away from the hitching post. "Well, if everything goes right, then you don't need to know what I am talking about, Mr. Jenkins. If anything goes wrong, you won't have time to wonder what I'm talking about. Do you understand that?"

Mr. Jenkins looked puzzled. "No, I can't say that I do, but then I don't reckon that it matters because I can't see what can go wrong." His face suddenly looked perplexed. He snapped his fingers. He said, "Oh, one thing I forgot to tell you. There will be a man wearing a white shirt standing out somewhere around that house. At least that's what they told me. That's the man I don't want to deal with, so if you have any trouble, it could be with that man. He's expecting someone coming to fetch that horse."

Longarm said, "White shirt, white house, red roof, gray barn. All right, Mr. Jenkins, you take it easy." Without another look he began spurring his horse down the road toward the International Bridge that led to Mexico.

As Longarm rode out of Nuevo Laredo toward the Monterrey Road, his mind was busy trying to guess exactly what Mr. Jenkins was up to. It wasn't the horse as he had previously thought. On the way across the bridge, he had stopped at the U.S. Customs Service and shown the papers to the officer on duty. He had confirmed that the certificates were genuine. So if it wasn't the horse, was it contraband of some kind, such as gold or silver or some other item that drew a high duty? But then, Mr. Jenkins had said that he, Longarm, could feel free to cast aside anything that he found in the saddle or the bags. So if it wasn't the horse and it wasn't contraband, what in hell was Jenkins trying to smuggle across? Longarm shook his head and smiled to himself. He guessed he had been a lawman for too long. Maybe the situation was just as Mr. Jenkins had said—he was a timid little fellow who was afraid of the ruffian he had bought the horse from and he didn't want to confront him again. It could be that simple.

But then, Longarm thought to himself, that had to be one hell of a horse to pay $140 in delivery charges. He didn't know many horses outside of the Kentucky racing horses that fetched the kind of price that you could add on $140. He shook his head. Well, there was one way to find out, and that was to go and fetch the horse, bring him back and then see what happened. Hell, he even reckoned he'd take the $140. It wouldn't make up for the hours of sleep he lost but at least it would be something.

He hit the outskirts of the little Mexican town and began looking for the Monterrey Road. It wasn't difficult to find since there weren't that many roads leading out of the place. As he jogged out of town on the roan, he was struck by how peaceful the place looked in the early afternoon sunshine. It was in stark contrast to so many times on the border when the only peace he'd known had been when he was taking time to reload. Mostly it had been gunfire and blood. The border was a deceptively quiet area, but Longarm was willing to bet that there was more devilment per square mile along there than any other place that he could think of on earth.

Like many towns, Nuevo Laredo was bounded by tumble-down shacks, nearly every one of which was white adobe with red clay tiles for roofing. He continued on. The shacks were mostly up close to the road, but then after he had gone on for a mile or so, he noticed, in the distance off to his right, one that was set back a ways from the road, perhaps half a mile. He touched the roan with his spurs and brought the horse up to a slow lope. He could see a small corral and he could see a weathered frame barn. From what Mr. Jenkins had told him, it looked to be the place. As he neared, he could see a figure or two in the yard of the house. There was a narrow path that turned in off the road and he rounded the corner and headed straight for the hacienda, fairly certain that he had found the right place.

It suddenly occurred to him, however, that he had neglected to ask Mr. Jenkins the name of the man that he was supposed to get the horse from—all he knew was that he was a man in a white shirt. White was a very common garment color in Mexico. As he rode toward the adobe hacienda, he could see that there were two Mexican cowboys, vaqueros, in the front yard sitting on cane-bottomed chairs and drinking out of a bottle that they were passing back and forth between themselves. He didn't much care for the sight of that. The last thing he needed was a fight with a couple of drunken Mexicans. Almost unconsciously, he put his hand to the butt of the .44 revolver at his side and lifted it slightly to loosen it from its holster.

Longarm rode into the yard. The two Mexicans stood up. Neither one of them was wearing a white shirt. He let the roan slacken to a walk, then to a slow walk, pulling him up a couple of yards short of the two Mexicans. He said to the older-looking of the two, though neither one was much over thirty, "I am looking for a man in a white shirt who has a horse."

The younger of the two, the one on Longarm's right, suddenly laughed. He said in good English, "Aw, señor. I have an excellent horse, but I am not wearing a white shirt. Is it necessary that I go put on a white shirt before we can do horse business?"

Longarm said, "Yeah, I reckon that did sound strange. Look here, I've been sent to pick up a horse. I've got the papers on him with the description. He's a black horse with a white blaze on his face and two white stockings on the front. He's branded with a big *HP* on his hip. Have I come to the right place?''

The younger man said, ''Aw, señor, yes, you are correct in your location. Please step off your horse and we will take you to the man who owns this horse.'' He suddenly smiled, flashing his teeth. He added, ''Aw, yes. That man is wearing a white shirt.''

Longarm paused before stepping off the roan. He took a few seconds to look the two men over with a fine eye. There was something not quite right about them. They did not look like vaqueros. They were too well dressed and they had a certain devil-may-care air about them. Both were wearing long-barreled revolvers by their sides. Longarm wondered if they could be pistoleros, but, he thought, if they intended to rob him, they were going after slim pickings. The journey to and from Mexico City had exhausted most of his cash reserve and he was down to only about fifty or sixty dollars. Of course, such a sum in a poor country might be considered enough to kill a man, but these two didn't appear to be that short of cash. Keeping a close eye on them, he swung his leg over the rump of the roan and stepped to the ground. The older of the two Mexicans stepped forward and took his reins. He said, in not quite the good English of the other, ''I will tie up this horse for you, señor. You go see the man who owns this other horse you come to seek.''

The younger of the two, who was also the slimmer, motioned his hand toward the white adobe hacienda. He said, ''The man who has charge of this horse you seek is inside. Come, we will drink a little whiskey. Then you can take the horse and go.''

Longarm walked slowly toward the white adobe building. It was an average-looking structure for that place. He figured it to be a four-room house with a cooking shack on the side. It was probably the property of someone who ran a few

21

cows or a few horses and did moderately well on what he could earn and what he could steal. Longarm had no earthly idea why such a valuable horse would be at such a location, but then, that was what he had come to Mexico to find out.

He reached the entrance with the younger Mexican to his left and slightly behind. The man said, ''Please step yourself forward into the *casa*, señor.''

The door was half open. Longarm pushed it the rest of the way forward and stepped into the interior. It was dim, lit only by the flickering glow of one lantern. After a moment, his eyes adjusted so he could see a table across the room from where he stood. Behind it, he could make out the dim form of a man wearing a white shirt. Looking closer, Longarm could see that the man was also wearing a broad-brimmed, flat-crowned border hat that appeared to be dark gray or white—it was difficult to tell in the light. He did note, however, that the hat supported a band of silver conchas. He could see the light reflecting off their delicate work. Just then, the younger Mexican said from behind him, ''Step forward, señor, to please yourself.''

Longarm took two steps forward, his eyes still on the man behind the table. The man had not spoken. In the dim light, Longarm could not tell if he was Mexican or Anglo. He was about to say something about the horse when he suddenly felt something very hard, very much like the barrel of a gun, being pressed against his spine in the small of his back.

The voice of the Mexican who had followed him in said, ''Be very careful, señor. *Tiene quidado.* Have care. This pistol, she explodes very easy.''

Longarm stook stock-still, making no motion with his hands. He had no doubt that he was about a hair trigger away from having his backbone blown in two. He felt a hand at his side and felt the weight of his revolver being removed.

The Mexican said, "Now, put your hands high, señor. Very high."

Longarm lifted his hands to the height of his head. He said, "If you're planning on robbing me, mister, you ain't going to get very much."

The Mexican said, "Now, señor, it is necessary that you lay down on the floor. I am sorry it will get you dusty, but you must lay facedown on the floor. Do you understand?"

"I understand, but that don't mean that I'm much going to do it," said Longarm.

The response brought a sharp jab with the barrel of the pistol. The young man said, "Señor, there are two guns pointing at your back. Now lay down on your face on the floor and put your hands behind your back. This is *necessario*."

Longarm's mind was racing but he wasn't coming up with any answers. He said, trying to see just how determined the men were, "I'll be damned if I'm going to lay down in this dust and put my face in it."

The words were no sooner out of his mouth than a loud explosion filled the air and he felt a rush of heat and powder go past his ears. The sound of the shot rang so loudly that, for a second, Longarm felt deafened.

The voice behind him said quietly, "Señor, the next time you don't move, I'm going to hit you over the head very hard and then you will be on your face."

Chapter 2

Longarm said, "Well, hell, if you're that damned set about it, I don't want you to go wasting any more ammunition shooting holes in the ceiling. I'll get down." As carefully as he could with his hands still up, he gingerly lowered himself to his knees and then went to all fours and then lay prone on the dusty floor.

A voice above him said, "Now, put your hands behind your back."

It was an effort lying as he was, but Longarm managed to get both hands to his back. Instantly he felt the steely clamp of a pair of manacles being fastened to each of his wrists. He wondered vaguely if they were the same irons he had used on Earl Combs coming back from Mexico City. He doubted it since they were in his room, as far as he knew, at the hotel that he had never stopped at, the hotel where he was going to get that much-needed sleep. Well, here he was on the floor of a cabin in Mexico. Maybe he'd just sleep there. But he said, "Boys, I don't know what you want with me, but I only have about fifty bucks on me. Now, if you want the money, take it, but it ain't worth killing me over."

Longarm heard a sudden laugh—it was different from the Mexican's—and then a voice said from somewhere else in the room, "Oh, we have no intention of killing you. You're much more valuable to us alive."

It was clear to Longarm the man who had just spoken was not a Mexican. He had a Southern accent, but other than that, Longarm could make nothing more of the man's voice.

Longarm said, "I don't know who you are, fellow, or who these other fellows are and I sure as hell don't know what you want with me. I'm just an ordinary shitkicker passing through your part of the country. A man in town hired me to come out and fetch back a high-priced horse for him. Said he was scared of the fellow he had bought the horse from."

By now, Longarm could tell from the direction of the laugh that it was coming from the man seated at the table. The man said, "Oh, now, Mister United States Deputy Marshal Custis Long, better known as Longarm to his friends and enemies alike, I think you can do better than calling yourself just another shitkicker cowboy, don't you reckon?"

Longarm felt himself go slightly cold inside. In his years as a lawman, he reckoned he had made more than his fair share of enemies. The only question in his mind was just how deadly this particular one was. There was little doubt in his mind that he'd walked into a carefully planned trap, but lying facedown on the cabin floor with his hands manacled behind his back left him with very few options. He could only wonder what the man at the table's intentions were. He said, "Look here, mister. I don't know what you're up to but I can guarantee you that mishandling a United States deputy marshal ain't exactly the way to guarantee yourself a long life, if you take my meaning."

The man at the table laughed pleasantly. He said, "Oh, Mr. Long. Let's don't kid each other. No one knows where you are. You haven't even reported in yet. The last people who saw you were the lawmen you handed Earl Combs over to. Since then, you've been out of sight. You haven't sent a telegram, you haven't written a letter. All you've done is go into a hotel, get a room, and then go over to the saloon and dig into a bottle. Nobody knows where you are, what you're up to, or who's got you. Now, to use your expression, isn't that about the size of it?"

Longarm raised his head as best he could under the strain his body was in and turned it toward the table. All he could make out in the dim light was the outline of the figure. He asked, "Mister, what have you got against me, exactly? Have I done you some wrong you think was unfair? I'm a deputy marshal and my job is to catch folks who break the law. Now, if you've been in the law-breaking business, and certainly you are breaking the law right now by what you are doing to me, then I don't see where you've got any kick coming if I threw you in the clink. But have I ever treated you unfair?"

The man said, "Marshal, that's a very nice speech and I'm not going to answer the question for you."

Longarm said, "You are making a mistake here. You just don't handle a deputy marshal like you're handling me. What makes you so damn sure that I am Custis Long, Longarm as they call him?"

That brought a laugh from the man at the table. He said, "Chulo, check his pockets and locate his badge. I've been told he carries it in his shirt pocket when he's not wearing it."

Longarm felt rough hands suddenly at work around his shirtfront. He felt a hand dig in between his chest and the dirt floor, the fingers going inside his left shirt pocket where

26

he carried his badge. In a second the badge was out. He could hear the mumbling. He said, "You better damn well be careful with that badge. I've been carrying it a good long time and I don't expect to lose it in some damn shack outside of Nuevo Laredo, Mexico. You got that?"

The man who had a surprisingly cultured voice said, "Now, Marshal, you shouldn't concern yourself about such matters. I can see that this is the famous Longarm badge. Of course, we never had any doubt that it was you, you understand? We've had our eye on you for a good long while. Let me compliment you, Marshal. You're a man who strictly sticks to his job. You're a dutiful man, Mr. Long. A credit to your service."

Longarm raised his chin and said, "Well, I wish I could say the same for you, Mister . . . whatever your name is. But I can guarantee you one thing. You're inviting the whole of the United States government to come looking for you. You don't capture deputy marshals and get away with it."

The man laughed slightly again. He said, "Oh, Marshal Long. The last time you were seen was at the Customs Service and all they saw was you heading south into Mexico. Where you were going or what you were up to, they won't be able to say, and neither will anyone else. But don't worry, your absence will be reported shortly."

Longarm raised his head again. He asked, "What the hell is your name? Who are you anyway?"

The man said, "Oh, why don't you just call me Mr. Brown. That should do for the time being. You've already taken the name Jones so I'll have to take something different. We'll make it Bob Brown. How's that suit you?"

Longarm said, "Well, I can't see you so I can't identify you, but your voice is somehow familiar. I can't place it but I have an idea that I will, given enough time."

27

"What makes you think that you'll have that much time, Mr. Jones?"

"I don't know, Mr. Brown. I reckon you could say that I'm hoping."

Mr. Brown laughed. He said, "All right, Chulo. You and Miguel get the marshal to his feet and blindfold him. I reckon it's about time we moved out."

Mystified as to their intentions, Longarm allowed himself to be wrenched and lifted to his feet. He made no protest, though being hauled up by his arms while they were bound behind his back was a painful process. He stood stock-still as a cotton bandanna was passed across his eyes and then knotted at the back. He said, "Mr. Brown, you all seem to have gone through a considerable amount of trouble. I figure this whole play must have started with Mr. Jenkins or else you wouldn't have known that I had called myself Mr. Jones to him. I guess you've had word from him?"

Laughing, Mr. Brown said, "Well, we've tried to dot all our *i*'s and cross all our *t*'s, Mr. Long."

Longarm said, "The only thing I can't figure out is what you want from me. I told you, I only have forty or fifty bucks in my pocket and the horse I'm riding doesn't even belong to me. You've gone through a hell of a lot of trouble, for a reason I can't divine."

"Why don't you leave the thinking to me, Marshal Long? We'll get along much better that way."

Longarm felt himself being turned and then forced forward. As he passed through the doorway, he could tell he had come back out through the front door. He heard Mr. Brown giving instructions to the two Mexicans to help him mount the roan. It was an awkward process for him and made possible only by the strong arms of the two Mexicans who, by now, he thought of as pistoleros.

Once in the saddle, Longarm sat quietly listening to the

creaking of other saddles as the men in the party mounted. Then he felt the motion of the horse and he could tell that someone had taken his mount on lead. At first, they went in a shambling walk, and by the turn they took, he could tell they were headed back toward the Monterrey Road. He said, "I don't guess anybody is going to tell me where the hell we are going, are they?"

"Marshal, I'll give you a piece of advice and it won't cost you anything. There is no use in your fretting your head about what is going to happen. If things go smoothly, you'll be all right. If not . . . well, I can't answer for the matter."

"Well, if you've a mind to murder me, I don't see why you don't get on with it right here and now. Why the hell do we have to ride off to some godforsaken place where they might not find my body for a while?"

Mr. Brown laughed. "Maybe that's the idea, Marshal Long."

"Yes, I reckon I could see the sense in that. Drop me off in some canyon way back in this wild country. It would be a spell before word got back to Denver that the U.S. marshal service was short one deputy marshal."

Mr. Brown said, "This may be no comfort to you, Marshal Long, but we actually have no plans to murder you. Not unless we have to, that is."

Longarm said, "Then what the hell are you doing with me? You've gone through considerable trouble to trap me over here, and now that you've got me and there ain't no chance of me getting loose, I don't see where it matters a lick to you whether I know what's to come or not."

"All in due time, Marshal. All in due time."

"Just tell me this: Are you some enemy of mine? Have you got a grudge against me? I'd like to at least know that much."

Mr. Brown said, "To tell you the truth, I've only barely

seen you on maybe one or two occasions, at least before this situation. I've heard of you, but you and I have never crossed swords.''

"Then are you working for somebody who does have a grudge?''

Mr. Brown said, "Marshal, you are full of questions, aren't you?''

Longarm said, "Well, if you were riding a horse that was being led and you were blindfolded and manacled by a bunch of strangers, don't you reckon that you'd have some questions?''

Mr. Brown said, "Well, I guess there is merit in that, Marshal Long. I suppose you do have a point. Unfortunately, it's a point that I'm not going to make clear for you. Not just yet.''

It was very difficult sitting the horse with his hands manacled behind him. To keep his balance, he had to lean forward as best he could. To make matters worse, the roan had none too smooth a gait. About then, he felt the horse turning to the right, and from the sound and the feel of the horses' hooves in the dirt he could tell that he had turned onto the Monterrey Road. Since they had turned to the right, he knew they were headed south. Now the pace quickened as the horses were lifted into a fast walk, almost a trot. It was almost all Longarm could do to keep his balance in the saddle. Just as he was certain that he was about to pitch off to one side, he felt a steadying hand on his shoulder. He said, "Hell, can't you at least tie my hands to the saddle horn? This is a hell of a way to ride. Besides that, my shoulders are fixing to start aching any second now.''

Mr. Brown said, "Not to fret now, Marshal. I reckon you've stood a little pain in your time. But right now, we've got to make some time. It'll be dark in another three or four hours and I'd like to get to where we are going before then.''

Longarm said, "But why can't you at least tie my hands to the saddle horn or something? It's hell riding like this."

Mr. Brown laughed shortly. He said, "Out of respect, Marshal Long, I think your hands ought to stay right where they are. I've heard stories about you that, if they were true, made you out to be some sort of magician. We'll hold you in the saddle, but you're going to have to stand the pace."

With that, Longarm could feel his horse being pulled forward, first into a trot and then into a slow lope. Only by putting all of his weight on the balls of his feet in the stirrups could he maintain his balance. He was leaning so far forward that if the horse were to suddenly slow down or stumble, he knew he would pitch right over the animal's head. He said, "Mr. Brown, I perceive that you are a cruel man. This is no way to treat a fellow human being."

Mr. Brown said, "I'm sorry for the inconvenience, but we've got no choice. I'm working on a pretty tight schedule."

"You said something about three or four hours. Do you mean to tell me I've got to ride like this for that long?"

"Not to worry, Marshal, you'll go numb pretty quick and you won't feel a thing."

Longarm said, "Well, hell, the least you could do is give me a drink."

Mr. Brown said, "Be glad to give you a drink, we just don't have time to stop for it."

"Are we heading to catch a train?"

This time there was no answer, only the steady drumming of the hooves of the four horses. Now he knew that there was a rider on each side holding him by the shoulders to keep him in the saddle. He assumed the third member of the party, supposedly Mr. Brown, was up front leading his pony. Mr. Brown might have been right that his arms and shoulders would go numb, but such relief was not coming. They were aching and cramping and his wrists were being chafed by the steel manacles.

How long they rode along the road, he had no idea, but then abruptly they began to slow and made a turn to the right. Now he could tell they were going into rough country. Occasionally he could hear the clink of an iron horseshoe on a rock, and then the country began to rise, then drop and rise again. Each motion caught him off guard and without the supporting hands he would have been thrown from the saddle.

Longarm asked, "Where the hell are we bound for? We are, for certain, out in the rough country."

There was no answer. The horses had been brought down to a walk now, but it was a hard forced walk and he could tell that they were winding their way down through rough and broken country by the way they turned left for a distance and then right and then back to the left. He could feel the terrain rise and fall and rise and fall. It seemed to him that the general incline of the land was upward. There were hills south of Nuevo Laredo, he knew, and he expected that they had passed into them and were winding their way through the peaks and valleys. He didn't know how much time had passed, but he knew the sun was falling low in the sky. The air was cooling. It wasn't long before dusk. By now, he had grown numb through the shoulders and upper chest. It wasn't exactly a relief but it was better than the sharp ache he had borne through most of the ride.

For the last hour or so no one had spoken, even when he'd asked a direct question. It was as if, by their silence, they were further obscuring the trail to the place where they were leading him. He had asked several times for a drink of whiskey but no one had answered. The only sounds he heard were the creak of saddles and the clink of horseshoes and the occasional snort of a horse. He wasn't actually afraid, but he felt he had no control of his own destiny. They had taken him so suddenly and so unawares so that he had no insight into the minds of the men who were leading him to an uncertain fate somewhere. Where, he knew not. The combination made him slightly nervous but he kept reminding himself that he had been in tight places before and he had always managed, somehow, to get free and to come away mostly unharmed.

It seemed they had reached a level place, at least for the last fifteen minutes or so as the horses had been walking on flat ground. He asked, "Are we nearly there?"

No one answered.

"Ya'll aren't exactly the most talkative bunch I've been around."

No one answered and no one laughed.

Longarm lapsed into silence after that. A slight breeze had sprung up and was blowing directly into his face, leading him to believe they were headed west now since a westwardly wind was the generally prevailing breeze in that part of the country at that time of the year. He calculated in his mind that they must have gone some ten to fifteen miles south and then curved around west another two or three. He had no idea how much farther they were going to travel. Behind the blackness of the blindfold, it was impossible to tell if it were night or day but he had the impression that full dark had not come.

As he was giving thought to what he could do, the party abruptly stopped. For a moment, they were marching along on horseback and then next they were dead-still. It felt curious to Longarm. His body felt as if he was still riding forward even though his brain told him they had come to a stop. A moment later he felt hands taking hold of him, pulling him out of the saddle. When they stood him on his feet, he was unsteady and almost lost his balance, but quick hands held him upright. The Mexican to his right said, "Now you walk, please."

His legs felt numb from the hips down and they had to half carry him as he stumbled along in the direction they indicated. After ten yards or so, they brought him to a halt and one of them told him to step up with his right leg. He did so as best as he could, half stumbling up what he took to be a set of steps. He felt hard tile or rock beneath his feet and he guessed he was on a porch of some kind. He was walked forward three more paces and then he heard a door creak open. From the sound, it was a big heavy wooden door. He was pushed through and then he felt smooth hard tile under the soles of his boots. They started him forward again, and as the circulation gradually returned to his legs he was able to walk without the fear of turning an ankle. They walked ahead for what he took to be five or six paces, then turned him to the right, then the left for another few paces and then finally back to the right again. He could tell, even through the blindfold, that he was in a dark place. It seemed to him to be a big empty house of some kind. After a walk through what he took to be a long hallway, they stopped. He could hear the sound of a key being fitted into a lock and then he could hear the sound of another heavy door opening. He was pushed forward. The hands holding him let go and he stumbled and almost fell to his knees. In time, he recovered and then stood there, not certain what to do.

Behind him, Mr. Brown suddenly spoke for the first time in a long while. He said, "Marshal Long, I'm sure you've got a lot of questions, but I'm afraid you're not going to get many answers. We're going to hold you in this place for however long our plan takes. I want you to know that we are going to do our best to treat you as well as we can. You'll be given good food, good whiskey. You'll be allowed to keep your smokes and your matches. You'll have a good

34

bed. There's a couple of windows through which you can get fresh air." Mr. Brown laughed slightly. "The air will come in but you can't go out. As I said, we are going to do our best to keep you as comfortable as we can. I don't know how long this confinement will last, that's not going to depend on me. We'll even furnish you with a woman, if it gets down to that."

Longarm asked, "Mr. Brown, you have me confused as hell. Just what are you holding me for? What do you hope to gain by keeping me in confinement, as you call it, here?"

Mr. Brown answered quietly, "We are going to try to arrange with the proper authorities in the United States to swap you for Earl Combs."

Chapter 3

The words so caught Longarm off balance that he involuntarily took a step backward and almost fell over. A quick hand caught him in time and steadied him on his feet. With astonishment on his face, he asked, "Brown, have you lost your damn mind?"

Mr. Brown said, "I don't think so."

Longarm said, "I can tell you right now that the United States government, and especially the federal bank, is not going to swap one U.S. deputy marshal for a man that embezzled two hundred thousand dollars."

"Well, we think different, Marshal. You've got quite a reputation. You're a well-known man and we expect this information to get into the newspapers and create quite an uproar. We think the government will see their way clear to trading Earl Combs for you."

Longarm said, "If you didn't sound so damn serious, I'd bust out laughing."

Brown said, "Oh, you can depend on it, Marshal. We're serious. Dead serious."

Longarm grimaced "When you say 'dead,' I reckon that you're talking about me."

Mr. Brown said, "We hope it doesn't come to that, Marshal. We'd much rather have Mr. Combs back because Mr. Combs knows where he hid the two hundred thousand dollars. We'd much rather have the money than you, as you can well understand."

Longarm shook his head sadly. He said, "You haven't got a chance. There is no way in hell the United States government is going to make a trade like that. Hell, the village idiot on his first horse trade would know better than that. No, sir. You've got the stick by the wrong end. Those folks are going to die laughing at you."

"Well, I guess we'll just have to wait and see."

Longarm asked, "What are you going to do when they tell you to go to hell?"

Mr. Brown paused for a second and then said coolly, "I guess we'll start sending them pieces of you."

Now Longarm paused. "What exactly do you mean by that? Pieces of me?"

"Oh, I guess we'd start with a finger, maybe an ear. Work our way through your easily severed parts."

The thought struck a tiny cord of fear inside Longarm, causing an involuntary shiver to run up his back. He could face bullets with much more equanimity than the idea of being held down and having a finger sheared or cut off. He said, "Brown, you don't sound to me to be that kind of man. I can't see you carving up a fellow and then sending him through the mail."

Brown said, "Well, we'll just have to wait and see about

that, Marshal, or at least you will. I already know what I am capable of doing."

"Why the hell did you pick me? Why didn't you pick a United States senator or something?"

Brown laughed. "You were handy, Marshal. We've been with you all the way from Mexico City looking for our chance but you never gave us one. We had to wait until you had turned Earl Combs over to that other marshal who was too well reinforced to attack."

Longarm said, "So, this is the plan you came up with?"

"That's about it. Now look, we're going to take the manacles off you and then we're going to lock the door. You will quickly discover there is no way out of this room. You can try to escape all you want but I don't believe that you will be successful. After a while, someone will bring you some supper and a bottle of whiskey and some smokes if you haven't got them. You'll be given your instructions on how to act when your food and other articles are brought to you. Be sure you obey what you're told to do. I'd hate to have to hamstring you or cut your ankle tendon. Do you understand?"

"I understand you're crazy."

Brown laughed. Longarm could hear footsteps receding, the sound of spurs faintly jingling against the hard tile floor. As the sound of Brown's withdrawal slowly faded, Longarm could feel someone at work on the manacles. He stood still, waiting. Finally, he felt his wrist come free of the steel, but for a moment his hands remained where they were. His arms and shoulders were so numb and stiff that he had to make a conscious effort to swing his hands forward to his sides. For another half moment, he didn't move at all. Then he heard the sound of the heavy door shut behind him, heard the sound faintly of a key being turned in the lock and the sound of footsteps going back down the hall, growing fainter with each second. Then there was nothing but silence. He reached up carefully and took the bandanna blindfold from his eyes. He thought he was as tired as he had ever been in his life. He had expected that the sudden light would hurt his eyes, but the room was dim enough so that his eyes adjusted fairly quickly from their enforced disuse.

He looked slowly around his prison. It was a handsome enough room: white walls, whitewashed, with a few pictures hung on the walls. There was a big double bed set in the middle of the room against the far wall. Beside that, there was a table with a kerosene lamp and on another table he could see a pitcher and a basin full of water. To his right, there were two windows in the side walls but they were really casement windows. They were high up and small and each one was barred with heavy wooden rods. Even if there had been no bars, he would not have been able to get through the windows anyway. They were too small, but they did serve to show him that the adobe limestone walls were at least two feet thick. The room had a ceiling formed by beams and plaster. He doubted a man would be able to dig his way either through the ceiling or through the walls.

But for the time being, all he wanted to do was to sit down and rest his aching body. He walked slowly toward the bed and sank down on it, grateful for its softness. He was sore but he knew he was going to be a lot sorer the next day. He took his hat off, then his boots, and then he sat there trying to figure out what kind of mess he had gotten himself into. To him, the greatest danger was this Mr. Brown's optimistic view that the United States government would be willing to swap an embezzler for a deputy marshal. Longarm knew as well as he knew his own name that the government did not operate in such a fashion. Deputy marshals, even ones that might be famous, were a dime a dozen. It wasn't every day that you caught somebody who had managed to embezzle

39

two hundred thousand dollars from the Treasury Department and then managed to get out of the country. He smiled wryly to himself as he thought of the reception Mr. Brown's proposal was going to draw from the federal banking system.

He lay back on the bed staring at the beamed ceiling, the wood dark against the white plaster. He didn't reckon there was any way out of this particular dungeon except through the door he'd entered. He didn't reckon it was going to be an easy trick to get through it. The door was probably guarded, and if it wasn't guarded, it was barred on the other side, even if he could somehow get past the lock. The windows were out, the ceiling was out, the walls were out, and he imagined that the floor was about as solid as the rest of the outfit.

He got up off the bed and limped slowly over to the table where the pitcher and basin rested. A couple of glasses sat beside the basin and he could see water in the pitcher. He poured himself a glassful and drank it down. When that was gone, he had another. It didn't do much for the hole that was located where his stomach should have been, but the water made a better meal than worry at any rate. He filled the glass again and then took it with him as he went back to the bed. There were a couple of chairs in the room, but they didn't look as comfortable as the bed. This time he sat up at the head, propping a couple of pillows behind his back.

He sat there slowly sipping at the glass of water, trying to think. He knew it was a useless process. For the moment and maybe for the next couple of days, he was going to be too tired and weak to do much about his situation, even if there were something that he could do. He reached into his pocket and rustled around until he found a cigarillo. There were matches by the lamp and he struck one and first lit his cigarillo and then the lamp, trimming the wick so that it threw off a nice glow to brighten up the room as the sun went down outside.

Brown's ignorance frightened Longarm. He wondered how long it would be before the man finally realized that the federal government was not going to trade out. Once they got such practice started, it could go on forever. Longarm knew what was going to happen. His worry was how long it was going to take Brown to figure out he had nothing to gain by holding a United States deputy marshal. And as for Brown talking about sending in pieces of his body, he thought the man surely wasn't that insane. For instance, if they sent in his little finger, how would Brown expect the authorities to know that it was Longarm's little finger and not the finger of some drifter off the street that they dragged in and gave the chop to? Aloud, he said, "Hell and damnation. This is a hell of a mess."

He was beginning to revive slightly and he puffed furiously at his cigarillo, sending up large clouds of blue smoke, trying to think. After a moment, he realized it was clear he didn't know enough about the situation to come to any kind of useful conclusions. The best thing was to rock on along for a couple days until he could spy out some opportunities. What form they would take he didn't know, but he did know that if a man was alert and on his toes, something usually turned up.

Right then he figured the best thing he could do was to try and get himself into as good a physical shape as he could, and that meant some supper and a few drinks of whiskey. He got up off the bed and limped over to the wooden door. He banged on it, partly to get attention and partly to find out how thick it was. He found out it was plenty thick, thick enough so that he regretted pounding on it so hard. After a few more licks with the flat of his hand, a little peephole suddenly opened in the door about head high. It surprised

41

him because it was so cunningly concealed in the curlicues and scrolling on the door. He could barely see the face of one of the Mexicans. It appeared to be the younger one, whose head did not quite come up to the level of the hole. The pistolero said, "Yes, señor, what do you wish?"

Longarm said, "Well, first of all, I want some supper, then I want a bottle of whiskey. Then I want some cigars or some cigarillos, whatever you've got, and then I want to speak to Mr. Brown."

The Mexican said, "The supper, the cigarillos, the whiskey is okay. I don't know about Mr. Brown. I don't think he wants to talk to you."

Longarm said, "Tell him I've got a few things he needs to know. If he's going to go about this business, I want him, for my sake, to get it right. Now, you tell him I want to talk to him."

Longarm could feel more than see the Mexican shrug and then suddenly the peephole was shut and the door looked as solid as before.

It was a long wait, but at the end of it Longarm was given an idea about how he would be served and trusted. There came a knock on the door, he got up off the bed and went over and waited for the peephole to be opened. He could see the older Mexican's face. The man said, "When we come, señor, you go way yonder to the back of the room. Then you lay down on the floor and put your arms out and you make no move or we shoot you. You understand? You don't look up, you don't get up, you don't speak, you don't nothing. Okay? You understand?"

Longarm said, "Yeah."

The Mexican said, "You stay there until we tell you get up. Understand? We come pretty quick."

"Yeah," Longarm said, mimicking the Mexican's Spanish-accented English. "I understand."

42

He thought they were a good long time about it. He looked at his watch when they came in the room. It had been coming seven o'clock and now it was nearly eight. It had been a full half hour since he'd placed his order for food, whiskey, smokes and the presence of Mr. Brown. Finally, there came a faint rapping on the big door. He got up off the bed and walked over. Apparently the peephole didn't open from his side and they weren't going to open it from theirs. He yelled out, "What!"

A muffled voice said, "You go where we told you to go. You lay down on you face and you shut you eyes. Do not move, señor, understand?"

"Yeah," Longarm said disgustedly. "I understand. I've been to school. I understand English even if you don't speak it."

"You go."

"I'm going." He turned and walked to the far end of the room and lay down beside the bed, his face pressed against the cold tile, his arms spread out. He lay listening. He could hear the door latch being turned, then he heard the heavy door swing open. Then he could hear the sound of boots as at least one man and maybe a woman—by the soft sound of low-heeled shoes—could be heard. He heard the sound of furniture being moved and then came the smell to his nostrils of some kind of food. He couldn't tell but it seemed to be chicken or beef or maybe both. All he cared about was his visitors getting the hell out of his room and letting him have a meal in peace.

He heard the footsteps retreat and this time he was certain it was one pair of boots and someone in a pair of soft leather shoes. He heard the heavy door close and the key turning in the lock and then heard a thump that he took to be a bar being placed across the outwardly-opening door. Finally, he heard the tiny sound of the peephole being opened and a voice saying, "Okay. Go eat. You got whiskey, you got cigars."

Longarm got up off the cold floor. He yelled as the peephole was closing, "Hey! What about Brown? I want to speak to Mr. Brown."

The peephole reopened. The voice said, "You eat now. Maybe talk Mr. Brown later. Okay?"

"No, damn it!" Longarm swore. "I want to see Mr. Brown. I want to tell him a few things. Hell, you guys are fooling around with my life here!"

The voice said again through the peephole, "You eat. Maybe talk later."

The peephole shut.

Longarm said, "Damn, damn, damn."

The smell of food was too inviting. A table that hadn't been there before had been set up in front of one of the straight-backed chairs in the room. On top of it was a covered tray. He could see all kinds of dishes and he hurried across and lifted the cloth that covered it. There was a bottle of good whiskey and a steaming plate of something that he didn't quite recognize and a pot of coffee and a cup. There was bread and butter. There was another dish that he guessed was some kind of flan, Spanish custard that tasted like caramel. He didn't care. Right then, he would have eaten grubworms if he could have gotten some ketchup to put on them.

He had meant to loosen himself up first with a drink of whiskey but he was too hungry. He sat down in the chair and fell straight to on the main dish. It was some kind of mixture of chicken and beef and pork in some kind of a cream sauce with peas and carrots and he didn't know what all in it. All he knew was that it was larruping good, and once he got started on it, the only time he stopped was to butter a chunk of bread or to take a sip of coffee.

He finished the dish in a very short time and would have

eaten another if it had been available. As it was, he had to content himself with eating a dish of mashed potatoes full of jalapeño peppers and chopped-up onions. He had never had mashed potatoes that way but they came out pretty good. Whoever was doing the cooking was a pretty fair hand at it. It wasn't exactly Mexican food but it was a bit spicy and wasn't much like anything he had ever had before. He finished up by eating the caramel custard and then the last of the coffee. He poured himself a glass of whiskey and lit himself a cigarillo. Even in such a short time he could feel some of his strength returning as a result of the meal.

With his cigarillo drawing good, he sat there, sipping at coffee into which he had poured a little whiskey. It made a fine combination. A friend of his had once called putting whiskey in coffee a long sweetening and he had come to think of it that way ever since. He remembered that friend. He was dead now. His name had been Coy, Buck Coy, and he had been a fellow deputy marshal. But he had been killed four or five years past. He'd had a beautiful young wife named Molly whom Longarm had gone to comfort from time to time. In the end, she had found a way to comfort him perhaps more than he was helping her. She was a wonderful woman, and if he had ever thought of marriage, it would have been with Molly, but she had declared that she would never marry another law officer. She lived in a small house on the Oklahoma border outside of Wichita Falls, Texas. It hadn't been six months since Longarm had visited her. The memory of their lovemaking gave sudden rise to a rush of passion inside him. He fought it down. He was in neither the place nor the situation to be thinking such thoughts. If he was to get out of this mess, he was going to have to direct every one of his faculties to finding some sort of a key to either his prison or the people who controlled his prison.

As he sat turning the situation over in his mind, he caught

a slight movement at the door and turned his head in time to catch the peephole open. Mr. Brown's voice said, "You want to talk to me?"

Longarm got up quickly. "Hell, yes, I want to talk to you. I want to explain a few things about what you think you might be able to accomplish by using me."

Brown said, "All right. I'll listen to you, not that it will do you any good. Wait where you are for thirty seconds until I back down the hall. Then you can come and talk to me through the peephole."

Longarm did as he was told, and when he got up to the peephole, he tried to glance through to see if he could catch a glimpse of the man, but the hallway had been darkened. He could barely make out Mr. Brown's dim form.

Brown said, "All right. Start talking."

Longarm said, "First, one thing's got me curious. How come you're so damn careful not to let me see you? You've let me see these Mexicans but you keep yourself completely out of sight. You blindfold me, you sit in the shadows. How come?"

"For your own good, Marshal," Brown said. "There is a chance that you might recognize me. If you do get a look at me, I've got no choice but to kill you."

Longarm said, "Then you be damn careful that you hide yourself well. Where would I have seen you?"

"Did you want to talk to me about what I look like or do you want to talk to me about your situation?"

"I want to talk to you about my situation. Brown, you're going about this all bass-akwards. In the first place, they are not going to swap you an embezzler for a deputy marshal. In the second place, how are you going to prove to them that you've got me?"

Brown said, "You're going to write them a letter. That's the way they're going to know I've got you."

46

"Like hell I will! If I do something like that, I'd never live it down. Giving in to the demands of a common crook. Hell."

"Suit yourself on that score, Marshal," Brown said. "All the letter will serve to do is to confirm that I have you captured. It's only a method of speeding matters up. I'm going to tell them I have you and then I'm going to send them your badge along with a letter from me. That and the fact that you can't be found is going to be proof enough. A letter from you confirming the matter will simply hasten your release. I'm not asking you to beg them to go along with the swap— I know that you're not the kind of man to do that—but I am suggesting to you that you can cut your prison time down quite a bit by a little cooperation."

"Well, I tell you, they are not going to believe it and even if they do, they're not going to do anything about it."

"Oh, I'm quite sure they'll believe it, especially with your badge. Your badge is famous for the low number it has on it. Is that a result of your having been a marshal for a long time?"

"No, it's just the way it worked out. But your sending them the badge ain't necessarily going to prove to them that I'm alive."

Longarm could almost hear Brown shrug. Brown said, "If I can't convince them that you're alive, then there's not much point in keeping you alive, is there?"

"What do you mean by that?"

"I think a letter would convince them that you are alive and that you are being well treated. You savvy?"

Longarm thought for a long moment. "Hell, Brown. You've got me in a box here. I don't much care for it."

Brown said, "Make up your mind about that letter. I'll get some writing material in to you tonight. I'm leaving in the morning and will be sending off my demands to the federal court and the federal offices in San Antonio. You can send the letter or not, as you choose." He laughed slightly. "Hell, you might even be able to slip some clue by me as to where you are."

Longarm said, "Brown, you're a son of a bitch. You're going to end up regretting this."

Brown laughed. "Look, you're going to get pretty desperate for a woman in there, as long as you're going to be holing down that room. I know all about you and your women. I wouldn't give me too hard a time, not unless you want to get mighty uncomfortable as the days go by."

Longarm said, "Go to hell, Brown."

Brown asked, "Do you want to write the letter or not?"

Longarm thought for a moment. "I don't see what good it would do. If I write the letter to prove I'm alive, what's to keep you from killing me as soon as you get the letter in hand? Where the hell is the advantage to me in putting anything down on paper, other than to express my feelings about what a sorry son of a bitch you are and what a fool I've been. What's the advantage to me?"

Brown said, "You've got it wrong, Marshal Long. I have no desire in me to kill a member of the marshal's service. I know full well how close you people are and how you protect your own. I think I can do this very easily with that famous badge of yours—the one with the dent in it where it stopped a bullet that would have gone into your heart, the badge that is celebrated throughout the marshal's service. I think I can do that with your absence and the badge. I think a letter from you would serve to cut down on the time that you are going to be enjoying my hospitality. That's the only reason I suggest the letter."

Longarm said, "Why is it, Mr. Brown, that I don't necessarily feel inclined to believe your every word? Is there something about you that I don't like other than the fact that you have tricked me, trapped me, and thrown me into this jail cell?"

"Look, Marshal, you can make your custody as easy or as hard as you want. I expect you to try and escape but you won't be able to. This matter could take a week or six months. Personally, I'm prepared to wait it out. I won't be here. But I can tell you this, when it comes time to do you some favors, I am leaving orders as to how you are to be treated—the matter regarding a woman, for instance."

Longarm said, "I don't reckon I'd screw anything of yours with a mule's dick."

Brown laughed. "Oh, I think your tune will change as the days go by."

"One thing you're forgetting and that's this Mr. Jenkins. I was seen with him. It is a known fact that I was in Laredo, and the first place they'll start looking for me is in Laredo, and somebody is going to tell them that I was seen with this Jenkins fellow. When they find him, they'll find you. When they find you, they'll find me. Ever think of that? Might be in your best interest right now to ride away and leave this door open."

Brown smiled, though Longarm couldn't see it. He said, "Mr. Jenkins never saw me. He's not part of my organization. He's nothing but a down-on-his-luck cardsharper, a small-time confidence man. We used him to catch your interest. He was given a very specific set of instructions to follow. The business about the horse—we thought you would suspect some sort of criminal activity and you'd take the bait. Guess what, Marshal? You took the bait and that's why you're here. There never was a horse. By now, Mr. Jenkins is in New Orleans or Phoenix or Tombstone or Kansas City or Houston. Trust me, he's no longer in Laredo."

Longarm said, "He's probably six feet under."

"There's that consideration, too. Marshal, I've talked to

you as long as is necessary. I'll have some writing materials slid under the door. Someone will come and collect the letter. If you don't write it, that's your business. You do what you want on that score. You won't be talking to me for a while, but there will be plenty of people around here to take care of you. I say adios to you now and I'm off."

Longarm said, "Hey! Wait a minute, damn it! Hold up there, Brown. I've still got a few things I want to tell you, you son of a bitch."

But he could tell from the hollow sound on the other side of the door that Brown had already left. He was alone in the big empty room.

He walked over to the table and poured himself a glass of whiskey and went over to the bed and sat down. He stared at the wall as he sipped at the liquor. For one of the few times in his life, he found himself totally baffled about what to do, what his next step should or even could be. There didn't seem to be a next step. For a moment, Longarm felt the slightest twinge of desperation, but with an effort he fought it down. This was one time when he was going to have to be at his best and do his best thinking. Brown was dangerous because he was so intelligent. He was deadly because of his intelligence and he didn't seem to have a conscience. He had willfully captured a United States marshal and was holding him for extortion. That took nerve and a lack of either conscience or good sense. Longarm wasn't sure which.

Chapter 4

For a long time, Longarm stared down into his glass of whiskey. He wasn't so sure that he wanted to leave the place alive. It might be for the best if Brown just killed him. He thought he would rather be dead than face Billy Vail and admit to how easily he'd been suckered into such a trap. Whatever had possessed him, he still didn't understand, except it was his damn curiosity. He had been almost certain that Mr. Jenkins had been up to some crime. Yeah, he had been up to a crime, all right. He was stealing, but what he was stealing was a deputy marshal. The only smuggling he had done was to smuggle him, Longarm, into Mexico and right into the hands of Mr. Brown and his ambitious plan to get the government to give him an embezzler and, thereby, $200,000 of government money. That, Longarm thought, was really going after the golden goose.

After a while, he began to take stock of what he had on hand that he could use in some way to free himself. They had taken his gun but had left him his gunbelt. He slowly

51

unbuckled it, looking ruefully at the big silver concave belt buckle. Normally concealed in the concavity of the buckle would have been a .38-caliber derringer held in place by a steel spring. But on the train trip back from Mexico City, Earl Combs had given him so much trouble wrestling around and cutting up that he had been afraid the small gun would become dislodged and fall out. As a result, he had packed it in his valise. It was still in his valise, but that was back at his hotel in Laredo. Normally, he didn't carry cartridges in the loops on his belt. They were too heavy and made the whole affair too heavy. But he had eight for some reason in the loops in the belt. He looked at the big .44-caliber cartridges and wondered what good they were. Without a gun to fire them, they were useless. He laid the gunbelt on the bed and then began feeling through his pockets. He had the cash—he got it out and counted it. He had fifty-one dollars. He also had some loose change. Then he had a small pocketknife. Wasn't much use as a weapon, about all he could do with it was sharpen a pencil or maybe cut a thread off his shirt, but it wouldn't do in a fight.

He surveyed his assets with a feeling of hopelessness. It didn't appear he possessed a single weapon that he could use to free himself. He got up and walked around the room, looking for anything he might contrive to use to gain his freedom. The room was bare except for the bed, the two tables, the two chairs, the lamp and a few pictures and a small mirror on the wall. He supposed he could spill the coal oil out and set fire to it, but it damn sure wasn't going to set the thick plaster walls on fire and the big wooden beams were too heavy to burn even if they did catch on fire. All he would manage to do was to burn himself up. Quite frankly, he viewed the situation as hopeless. He could not remember ever feeling so helpless before in his life.

He sat back down, finished his whiskey, and poured more

into his glass. Just as he was taking a drink, he heard a scratching at the door. He glanced over and saw some white pieces of paper along with a pencil being shoved underneath. He got up, padded soundlessly over in his stocking feet—he still hadn't put his boots back on. There were two sheets of bond paper and the pencil. He leaned down, picked them up, walked back and laid them on the table where he had eaten his supper. He didn't know if he would write the letter or not, but as Brown had pointed out, it might speed things up, and there was also the chance that he could give whoever might read the letter some clue as to his whereabouts and his situation. He had nothing to lose by writing the letter except to make known his embarrassment, but that was going to come anyway. It was, he thought, a situation he was going to be a long time in living down.

After a while, he gave up thinking and decided that the best thing to do would be to sleep on the matter. He undressed down to his bare skin, which meant taking off his jeans, his shirt, and his socks—he didn't bother with underwear. After that, he pulled the covers down on the bed, poured himself half a glass of whiskey, climbed up and sat with his back against the headboard. There was a nice breeze coming through the two casement windows but it wasn't doing him a hell of a lot of good except to make the room comfortable.

After a moment or two, he lit a cigarillo, smoked that, drank the whiskey, turned down the lamp and slid down into the bed, pulled the covers over him and put his head on the pillow. He thought he'd have a hard time going to sleep but it seemed as if he had no more than shut his eyes when he went out like a light. He was a good deal more tired than he realized. He came awake the next morning to the sound of something at the door. He sat up alertly. It was already dawn and sunshine was streaming into the room. He recognized the sound at the door as someone working a key in it from the other side. Finally, the lock clicked back and then the door was pushed open.

To his surprise, Longarm saw a woman standing there holding a tray with steaming coffee and a dish of some kind of food. Without a look at him, she came shuffling forward and set the tray on the table where the remains of his supper still lay. At the door, one of the Mexicans who had accompanied them on the ride from Nuevo Laredo was leaning against the doorjamb, a revolver held in his hand. He looked sleepy and yawned as Longarm glanced his way.

Longarm switched his eyes back to the woman. She was wearing some kind of shapeless robe. He could tell very little about her, neither her age, nor much about what she looked like. Her hair was tangled and her face was without makeup. She could have been thirty or forty. He watched as she transferred the dirty dishes from the night before onto her tray and then set his breakfast on the table. He could see it was ham and eggs and biscuits along with a pot of coffee and a little pitcher of cream. He said to the woman, "Thank you, that looks good."

She barely gave him a glance as she turned and hurried back toward the door. Longarm watched her all the way. She didn't walk like someone who was old, she walked like someone who was ashamed. It seemed an odd way to put it even to himself, but that was the way she walked. In another second, she had scuttled through the door. The Mexican yawned again, pulled the door to, and then Longarm heard the familiar sound of the lock turning and then the bar falling into place.

Longarm sat up and swung his legs around and yawned. So he hadn't been dreaming, he thought. He was in this damned hole. His dreams had been about Molly Coy. He wondered if he would ever see her again or feel her skin or kiss her lips. He stopped himself quickly. It wouldn't do to let his mind run in that direction.

As he ate his breakfast, which was very good, his thoughts returned to the woman who had come hurriedly into his room. He couldn't quite figure her out. She wasn't Mexican. She was a white woman with very fair skin. He supposed her hair was a light brown, almost a tawny blond, but it was so tousled and jumbled that it was hard to tell. She had been wearing a blanketlike blue robe that was so bulky it hid her shape. But as she bent over to put his breakfast dishes on the table, he could tell from the look he got of her rear she was not fat or chunky. He had half an idea that the robe was concealing more than might be expected, but then he told himself it might also be that he had been too long without a woman and too long in this damn whitewashed room.

It was about an hour and a half later that the woman returned. Longarm was standing on a chair looking out one of the little casement windows. He turned and watched the door open as the woman scuttled in with a tray in her hands. She hurried to the table and began stacking his breakfast dishes on it. Longarm glanced at the door. The Mexican pistolero was there but he was lounging back against the wall outside the door and his gun was holstered. Longarm was wearing only his jeans. He was barefoot and shirtless. The woman worked quickly. She refilled his pitcher of water, took his bucket of slops, then picked up the tray full of dirty dishes and went out of the room as silently and as quickly as she had entered. He took note that he was not commanded to lie down on the floor.

He got down from the chair, his mind turning over and over. This mystery woman. She did not fit the part of a maid, especially in Mexico. He had no doubt that there were half a dozen native women around the ranch who could have been doing her function. It was a very strange state of affairs and one he intended to get to the bottom of, somehow. He sensed that he might be able to use the woman. But there was still the matter of the letter and whether he should write it.

He didn't know how the woman could help, and he didn't have the slightest idea when or in what manner, but she seemed to be the only tool that had presented itself. What he couldn't figure was the hangdog, ashamed, stooped look she had about herself. Someone had whipped that woman plumb to the ground, either in spirit or physically.

He walked over to the bare table and looked at the still-blank sheets of paper. He hadn't made up his mind about the letter and he knew he had better make it up pretty quick. As if someone was reading his mind, the peephole suddenly opened and he heard Brown's voice. He said, ''Marshal Long, have you got the letter ready?''

Without moving from where he was standing, Longarm said, ''No, not yet.''

''I'm leaving in an hour. You've got that long.''

''I'll study the matter.''

''It's entirely up to you.''

''I appreciate that information.''

The peephole was suddenly shut.

He sat down at the table and looked at the paper. It was a good heavy bond. Quality. He guessed Mr. Brown did all right for himself in more ways than one. He picked up the pencil, still undecided. He had spent a good deal of his waking time the night before trying to decide if he would write the letter, and if he did, what he would say. Now it seemed the time had come to make up his mind. He wet the end of the pencil and then leaned over the paper and began writing laboriously in a cramped style.

To Whom it may Concern:
    This letter is written by the hand of Custis Long,

United States Deputy Marshall, stationed out of Colorado—Billy Vail, Chief Marshal. This is to notify you that I have been captured and am being held prisoner by a son of a bitch who calls himself Mr. Brown. His intention is to get you to swap me for that embezzler Earl Combs. Mr. Brown is ignorant enough to believe such an idea is going to work. I have told him it's a foolish play but he won't listen. He says if you don't make this trade, he is going to start sending you small pieces of me. I take it by that he means chopping off a finger or a toe or something like that. I guess his intentions are to let you know that he is serious. If you make the trade, naturally I would be pleased and I would guarantee you that I would recapture Earl Combs and I would find the money, and I would take this Mr. Brown into custody in a pretty quick time. However, it is my opinion that Mr. Brown is going to kill me whether you make the swap or not. I'm being held somewhere in the interior of Mexico, and I will give Mr. Brown credit for knowing how to lock a fellow up without much chance of escape. Tell Billy Vail he can have a good laugh about how I so foolishly let myself get trapped. Ya'll can make up your own minds about what you want to do about this situation. I am going to try my best on my own to manage things at this end. That's all I've got to say.

The letter was signed. "Custis Long, United States Deputy Marshal."

When he was through, he sat back and took a moment to read what he had written. He'd made as much sense as he could out of the situation. He had told the folks at the other end what he thought. He didn't expect Mr. Brown was going to be too pleased about his statement that he figured he was a dead man either way, swap or no, but that was the way he saw it.

After he read the letter the second time, he couldn't see anything he wanted to change, so he got up, took the sheet of paper to the door and slid it under. Then he banged hard and yelled, "Here's your damn letter, Mr. Brown." After that, he walked back and sat down at the table and poured himself a drink of whiskey. So far as he was concerned, matters were now out of his hands, at least in the appeal-for-help department.

A moment later, he heard soft footsteps and then the sound of the paper rustling. A minute or two passed and then the peephole opened. Mr. Brown said, "That's quite a letter, Marshal Long."

Longarm said, "Glad you liked it, Mr. Brown."

"I rather resent your implying that I'm going to kill you one way or the other."

"Well, ain't you?"

"Why would I want to do that?"

"Because you can't afford to turn me loose. You know as well as I do that I'd spend the rest of my life looking for you."

Mr. Brown laughed. He said, "Yes, but you wouldn't know who or what you were looking for. You don't know what I look like, you don't know where I live, you don't know what I do. You know nothing about me, so you are wrong, Marshal, that I would kill you anyway. As I've told you, I have no desire to have the murder of a United States deputy marshal on my hands."

"Well, I'm not going to change the letter," said Longarm.

Mr. Brown said, "Then so be it, but at least I have more proof that I have you alive. In fact, I couldn't have improved upon the letter. It shows that I have you, it shows that you are in desperate straits, and it shows that you are in great danger. I think it will urge the gentlemen of the banking commission to speed their decision. What do you think?''

"I think you're a low-down son of a bitch."

Brown laughed again. "I'm leaving now, Marshal. Is there anything you want?''

"Not that you've got."

"Well, if you think of anything, just tell one of the boys. Even a woman. You're going to get awful lonesome and that is a very small room that is going to get a lot smaller. I'll be glad to provide you with all the entertainment I can."

Longarm said, "Just keep the whiskey and the good vittles coming. I'll think about the woman, but like I said, I don't want any of your hand-me-downs."

"That amuses me, Marshal, that you would think you and I have the same taste in women. I think you're rather putting on airs with that attitude."

Longarm said, through gritted teeth, "I'd like to put some airs on you."

"Well, I'm gone now, Marshal. Adios."

The peephole shut and Longarm could hear footsteps receding down the hall. Longarm said, "Shit!" and slammed his hand on the table. He didn't reckon he'd ever run across anybody so smug, so sure of himself, so irritating, so damnable as this fellow Brown and there wasn't a thing he could do about it. "Damn!" he said aloud. "Damn, damn, damn."

At one-thirty by his watch, the woman came back bringing his lunch. She had changed out of the blue blanket-material robe into another one. It was still a robe, but it was gayer in color, pink and white. It seemed to be quilted. Also, she had combed or brushed her hair and she looked considerably better. But her face was still devoid of makeup and she still walked as if she was ashamed of herself.

Longarm rose off the bed and walked over to watch her

set the dishes on the table. She'd brought him steak and potatoes and green beans with what looked to be apple cobbler for dessert. He glanced toward the door. The pistolero was not there, but Longarm could see him farther down the hall standing near a door some ten yards distant. He guessed it was a door that led back into the main part of the house. He had the feeling that he was segregated off in some sort of a wing of the house and that the only way out was through the door the pistolero was standing by.

Longarm brought his attention back to the woman. He asked, "What's your name?"

She gave him a scared look and shook her head. Then she picked up her tray and hurried out of the room with the same quick shuffling gait. She closed the door behind her and he heard the key turn in the lock, but this time he didn't hear the bar fall into place. He wondered if they were getting careless with Mr. Brown gone. Perhaps he should begin to watch for his opportunities.

The afternoon wore along slowly, the minutes seemed to pass like miles under a mule's feet. Longarm had eaten his lunch as slowly as he could, savoring the good food and reflecting that at least he was being fed well. He found himself looking forward to his next visit by the mysterious woman. He didn't know what time the regular hour was for supper, but it had been a late lunch, so he didn't calculate she'd come in with supper much before seven o'clock. He kept speculating about her, wondering who she was, where she had come from, what she was doing in such a place, wondering why she thought so little of herself. In her last visit, he had noticed that she had grayish-blue eyes. They hadn't been dulled, they had been bright, lively and intelligent. The woman was a mystery, and no mistake. He only wondered if she was a mystery he could first solve and then make use of—he was becoming desperate. He'd been in his cell, as he thought of it, not quite twenty-four hours and already he had realized that he couldn't take much more of it. He was careful about the whiskey. He had determined that he would drink only in the evenings, maybe one in the morning. It would be too easy to get drunk and not be able to take advantage of an opportunity when it presented itself. Lord, he thought, what he would give for a gun. Over and over, he berated himself for leaving his hide-out gun in his valise. If that damned Earl Combs hadn't been kicking up such a fuss, it would have all gone so much better. He'd have had the derringer and he could have gotten the drop on the pistolero and relieved him of his sidearm and then he would have seen how matters turned out. Mr. Brown might have gotten the surprise of his life.

The afternoon wore on. He had explored the room about as well as any room had been explored. In his stocking feet, he had stepped off the width and the length of the room and found out that it was about fifteen by eighteen foot. He'd looked under the bed, he'd looked behind the pictures. He had scanned every square inch of the tiled floor. There wasn't a weapon or an amusement to be had. He thought of tearing up the table, taking a leg from it, and trying to bash in the head of one of the pistoleros. But that wouldn't work because they had, apparently, taken the habit of staying away from the door now. They hadn't seemed concerned about the woman and that made him wonder. But he found himself counting the minutes, never mind the hours, until she would show up with his supper. About all that he could do to pass the time was pace back and forth. It wasn't the most enjoyable or the most enlightening hobby he'd ever practiced. And besides that, it was hard on his socks, but he knew better than to wear out his boot leather on such an activity. After a day of walking over the small square tiles, he had decided that the best description for a mean woman was that she had a heart as hard and cold as a Mexican tile. There were a few in his past that he could have laid that label on.

Finally, he saw the sun begin to drop. He hoped that supper was coming soon. He wasn't particularly hungry, but he was hungry to see the woman, hungry to pierce her mystery. It would probably turn out that there was no mystery. She was somebody's half-witted cousin who was given scullery work to keep her out of the way. But he didn't really believe that; there was too much intelligence in those gray-blue eyes of hers. It didn't really matter; she obviously had orders not to talk to him. All he would get out of her was a severe look.

When she finally came that night, it caught him off guard. He was lying on the bed, half dozing, still wearing only a pair of jeans with no shirt. The sound of the lock being turned caught him just waking up. He rose to a sitting position, blinking drowsily as she came into the room. He was not so sleepy, though, as to not notice that she was no longer wearing the robe. She was wearing a long dress that fell down to her ankles. It wasn't a particularly pretty dress, nor did it fit her very well, but it was a vast improvement over the bulky robes. The dress was blue with small white print on it and it was a thin enough material so that he could see her shape beneath it. He didn't know if it was because he'd been without so long, but all he knew was that she looked mighty good to him. She went straight to his table and started unloading dishes. He could see that he was going to have fried chicken and creamed corn and mashed potatoes for supper that night along with a big glass of what he took to be iced tea and a pot of coffee. There was the same apple cobbler for dessert.

He got off the bed and took two steps toward her. She glanced up quickly at him. He said, "Don't be afraid. You don't have to be skittish around me."

She didn't answer. She looked back down at the table and began arranging the dishes in the proper order.

Longarm glanced down the hall. There was no sign of a pistolero on guard. He asked the woman, "What's your name?"

Without looking up, she gave him a shrug and said, "What does it matter?"

He was surprised that she had answered, he had been half afraid that she was mute. Her voice also surprised him. It was a cultured voice, not the voice of a woman who had known nothing but the rough frontier. There was no trace of a Spanish accent in it. He said, "It matters to me. I'm getting plenty lonely in here. My name, as I guess you know, is Custis Long. I'm a U.S. deputy marshal."

She still wouldn't look up. She said, "I know."

Longarm noticed that she had tied her hair back with a gay blue ribbon and wondered if she had done it for him. He asked, "Why don't you tell me your name. I'd like to be able to call you something."

She said, "I still don't see what it matters. We won't be talking that often."

"Humor me."

"All right, it's Sarah. Are you happy?"

Longarm laughed slightly. He said, "Happy? No. A little bit better off? Yes."

She picked up her tray. "I've got to go."

Longarm glanced again through the open door and down the corridor. He asked, "Where's your guard?"

"There's no need for one. The only door out of this part of the house is down the hall. You couldn't make it through that door. It leads into the main part of the house."

Longarm said, "Yeah, but what if I was to grab you around the neck so that you went to screaming bloody murder and took you as a hostage like they've taken me as a hostage. What about that?''

She laughed without mirth. She said, "It wouldn't make any difference.''

"What do you mean, it wouldn't make any difference?"

She said, "No one would care is what I mean. In fact, the man that you call Mr. Brown, if he were here, would probably be standing in the hall applauding you and urging you on.''

Longarm looked at the woman keenly. He said, "I take it that he's no friend of yours.''

"Friend?'' She laughed bitterly. "That's a joke.''

"You said the man that calls himself Brown. What's his real name?'' Longarm said.

She looked up at him with an amused look in her eyes. "I'm not ready to get killed yet. I don't think you can expect me to tell you that. I've got to go now.'' She clutched the tray to her breasts and began backing toward the door.

Longarm said, "Wait a minute. Could you at least bring me some books to read? Anything to pass the time. Hell, bring me an old deck of cards.'' He ran his hand over his face. "And this beard stubble is starting to itch. See if you can't get me a razor. Surely they don't think I can cut my way out of here with a straight razor. And I need a toothbrush and some salt and baking soda. Hell, my mouth feels like the inside of my boot.''

She said, "I'll see what I can do. I have no authority here, I'm just a servant.'' Then she backed through the door, closing it behind her. He heard the lock click and he was alone again.

Two long dreary days passed. The only bright spots were Sarah's visits when she came in the morning and then at lunch and at supper. She was a hard one to draw out, try as Longarm would. All he really got out of her was her name and that she worked at the hacienda. He tried to provoke her by asking what a white woman was doing in such a menial position, but she wouldn't answer him. She didn't refuse to answer his questions, she simply evaded them or remained mute. As best as he could, he tried to draw her out about conditions at the hacienda, such as how many men were there, where it was located, how far it was from the border. He had figured in his own mind, judging from the ride he had made, that it was about twenty miles from Laredo. He had asked her if this was true, but she didn't answer. She merely shook her head.

But one nice thing was coming from their growing acquaintanceship. She was dressing better. Now she was wearing clothes that set off her figure, which was even better than Longarm had originally thought. She was small-boned and tiny at the waist and appeared to have big breasts. It was the kind of figure that Longarm particularly favored. Looking at her, however, was causing feelings to stir that he couldn't afford. He had to keep his mind on his business.

One day at lunch, she brought him an unusual dish that was made from thin strips of chicken breast mixed in with slices of fresh tomatoes and cucumber and avocado. She had covered it with some kind of dressing that was tangy but creamy at the same time. He had never had anything like it before. He asked her who did the cooking, that he had never eaten such food in Mexico.

She shrugged. "I cook for you."

That explained a lot. He had expected the normal, greasy fare you got in Mexico, but the meals that he had gotten were cooked by someone who knew what cooking was and took pride in it. He said, "So, you're the cook on top of being the general servant around here?"

She shook her head. She said, "No, I only cook for you and for myself. The men who work here and the other women have their own cook. They don't like my cooking.''

He sat there at the table, staring up at her. He said, "Sarah, you know what they are doing to me is wrong. You know that the man who calls himself Brown is not going to get away with this."

"There's nothing I can do about it."

He said, "You could help me."

She got a sudden frightened look on her face and began backing toward the door. She said, "No! I'm afraid of this place. I'm afraid of all of them."

On the afternoon of his fifth day of captivity, he couldn't stand it any longer. He began banging on the door and kept on banging until, finally, the peephole opened and the young Mexican was visible there. He asked, "What you want, Señor Marshal?"

Longarm, hating to say the words, hating to be so weak, and especially hating to say them to this Mexican face, said, "Brown said I could have a woman. I want a woman. Send me a woman this evening."

Just as he had feared, the small man laughed, his voice high and shrill. He said, "So, now choo want a woman. Hah! You tell us, you don't need no woman. You strong. *Fuerte.* Now you tell us you got to have one. So, the rooster wants to crow."

Longarm said through gritted teeth, "Listen, Chulo, or whatever the hell your name is, either get the woman or don't. Just don't laugh like you've lost your false teeth. One way or the other, do something."

The Mexican's droll voice came back. He said, "Oh, I think you get a woman, all right. Yes, I think I know exactly the right woman for you. Yes, yes. You going to like her. You like snow? You like ice? We're going to send you a woman that will remind you very much of snow."

Longarm said, "Don't do me any damned favors, Chulo. Forget I mentioned it."

"You want the woman or not?"

Longarm clenched his teeth until his jaw muscles bulged out. He said, "Yes, damn it, I do. Send her after supper, after it gets dark."

The Mexican laughed again. He said, "Okay, Mister Big Shot Marshal. You gonna get this woman. We don't make no guarantees, though. Ha, ha, ha, ha, ha." The peephole shut.

Longarm suddenly thought of something and banged on the door again. The peephole opened up again. Chulo's voice said, "What? What you want now?"

Longarm said stubbornly, "I want a bath. Get a bathtub in here and let me get myself cleaned up. I've been wearing these same damn clothes for a week, at least I'd like to get my body clean."

"What choo think we running here? A hotel?"

"Listen, Brown said he'd treat me good. Well, that ought to include a bath. Get a bathtub in here and some hot water."

The Mexican mumbled for a minute and then said, "Okay, okay. But you better behave yourself. I think maybe you better let us have the razor before we bring that bathtub in there."

"I'll slide it under the door," Longarm said.

It wasn't much of a bathtub so it wasn't much of a bath, but at least Longarm was able to get most of the road dirt off himself and reduce the smell so he wouldn't run a woman off completely. When they took the bathtub out, they gave him his razor back and he shaved himself. He hated putting his dirty clothes back on now that he was clean, so he took a sheet and wrapped himself up with that. It was getting close to dinnertime and he was getting anxious to have the meal over with and have the woman sent to him. The meal itself was a surprise because Sarah didn't bring it. Instead, a Mexican woman came in with a kind of spiced-up stew and some rough bread and butter and some sliced onions and tomatoes. It was a far cry from Sarah's cooking. He tried to ask the Mexican woman what had happened to Sarah, but she either didn't understand his English or his attempts at Spanish. All she did was shake her head and said, "No say. No say. I don't know."

He ate quickly, pushing the food down, but even while he ate, he worried about Sarah. He wondered if they could have overheard him asking her to help him. He wondered if somehow he had gotten her in trouble. He also wondered if, perhaps, she was sent in to gather information as to what he was going to attempt. He hoped that was not true. He liked her. He felt sorry for her and there was also the mystery about her that he found intriguing.

Still wearing his wraparound sheet, he went and sat on the side of the bed, poured himself a whiskey, and lit a cigarillo. It was growing dim outside so he took a moment to light the lamp and trim the wick to a medium glow. Longarm sat there, anxious as a bridegroom, eagerly awaiting whatever kind of woman they were going to send him. He wondered if it was going to be the fat serving wench that had brought his supper. Hell, he would even take her. He was trying to think back just how long it had been. He had come back in from that two-week chase in New Mexico and then had been shipped out immediately to Mexico City. That had taken another ten days. Then he had been in this room for five or six days. Hell, he thought. He might as well have been a monk the way things were looking. It had been nearly a month since he'd dipped his wick.

His head suddenly swiveled around to his left as he heard the sound of a key in the lock. The door opened slowly and, in the dim light, revealed only the form of a woman. The door closed and she came walking softly toward him on her bare feet. As she came into the circle of the lamplight, Long-arm started. It was Sarah.

Chapter 5

For a second, he could only stare at her, confused. Finally he said, "What are you doing here?"

She shrugged. She said, "You asked for a woman. I'm a woman, sort of."

Longarm looked at her closely. Her hair was done and there was faint makeup on her face. She was wearing a thin wraparound robe. He said, "My Lord, Sarah. I never thought they would send you. I was thinking they'd send one of the Mexican girls around here."

She asked, "Aren't I good enough?" Her voice was low, dull.

Longarm said, confused and befuddled, "It's ... it's not that. You just took me so by surprise. I don't think of you that way. You're ... well, I don't know how to explain it. You seem more like a lady to me."

Sarah smiled faintly. She said, "One who goes around in an old blanket made into a robe? One who carries out your dirty dishes and your slop bucket? That seems like a lady to you?"

He was still trying to get his feet under him. He had stood up the moment she had come into the room. Now he clutched the sheet tighter around himself and said, "No, no, no. It's not that. It's just . . . I don't know how to say it, Sarah. You seem so dispirited, as if you had given up on everything. I could no more grab you and stab you than . . . well . . . I could see myself courting you, if you can understand that."

She said, "Well, I'm all you get. When Richard set off, he left orders that if you asked for a woman, it was to be me. So you either use me or do without. That's all I can say."

Longarm said, "Richard? Who's Richard?"

She smiled her faint smile. She said, "The one you call Mr. Brown. The boss. The big honcho. The one whose word is law. The maniac."

Longarm looked at her closely. He had noticed the bitterness that had crept into her voice as she talked about the man. He said, "You sound as if you know him mighty well."

"I do."

"Then why don't you tell me about him?"

She shook her head violently. She said, "No, thank you. This isn't much of a life, but at least it's better than being dead." She lifted her head and looked at Longarm. "What should we do? You'll give me great embarrassment if you send me away now."

Longarm sat back down on the bed. He said miserably, "Hell, I don't know what to do. What can I say?"

She said, almost smiling, "For one thing, you can tell me why you are wearing a sheet like a Roman senator."

Longarm said, "Well, I ain't never seen a Roman senator,

71

but I'm wearing the sheet because I've just had a bath and my clothes aren't all that clean. I didn't figure to put them back on once I was slicked up for the lady that was coming to see me.''

"I've never seen one either, only in drawings. But they wear something called a toga, which is the way you're wearing that sheet.''

Longarm laughed slightly. As he did he realized that it was perhaps the first time he'd laughed in several days. He said, "Well, I guess it's fitting then, if I recall what little I learned in my schooling about those Romans. They were always shutting one another up or else stabbing them with knives.''

She said, "We can't go on talking about Roman senators. Can't you change your mind about me?''

Longarm said, "I don't know. You just took me so by surprise.''

"Maybe this will help,'' she said. She took two steps closer to him and then untied the light robe and let it slip from her shoulders.

Longarm drew a soft, deep breath in spite of himself. The lamp light flickered off her pink and white body. She had exactly the kind of figure he liked. She was small-boned and much smaller naked than she had appeared in the bulky outfits she had been wearing. She had large breasts with big brownish-red nipples. The pubic hair that began at the vee of her legs was a curly light brown. He looked her over carefully from her straight legs to the little mound of her stomach up to her breasts and then up to her slim neck to her generous mouth and her wide, blue-gray eyes. Her hair was loose, framing her face, falling just below her shoulders.

He said huskily, feeling himself stir inside, "Why don't we get up here on this bed and lie by each other and see what happens.''

Without a word she crawled up on the foot of the bed and then made her way to the headboard, then turned over and lay on her back. Her eyes were fastened on the ceiling.

Longarm shrugged his way out of the sheet and then climbed up on the bed. He lay on his left side, looking down at her, his eyes still full of admiration. He said, with that husky tone he always got in his voice, "I don't know if anybody's ever told you, but you are one damned good-looking woman."

She said in almost a monotone, "I've heard it before but it's been so long, I've forgotten."

Longarm said, "You're not helping anything by laying there like a sacrificial lamb." He tried to make it funny but it didn't come out that way.

"I can't help it. It's been so long, I don't know if there's anything left in me." She turned her head toward him. "I want you to understand that I am glad this happened. I'm glad Richard did this. He thinks he is punishing me more, but he's not. This is a chance for me, a chance with a good man like you. I was getting so desperate, I was thinking about approaching one of the Mexicans. But then you were here and I heard them talking about a woman for you. I had hoped it would be me, but now that I'm here, I'm not sure what to do anymore. You'll have to help me."

Longarm sighed. He said, "Well, there's the rub, lady. I'm of two minds about this myself. I'm not sure I know how to go about stirring you up. My own fire hasn't completely been lit and I don't know where your coals are so that I can blow on them."

Now an almost pleading tone came into her voice. She said, "Just do it. Perhaps I will feel something and it will all come back to me. You must know that I haven't felt anything for a long, long time. I don't even feel like a woman anymore. I feel like this is my last chance and I'm asking you to please help me.''

Longarm's mind was still confused, but it seemed that he had no choice in the matter. He leaned over and kissed her on the mouth. Her lips were thin and dry. He pulled back. He said softly, ''Sarah, you're going to have to loosen up more than this.''

She said, ''I'll try but I'm very nervous.''

Longarm leaned over again, this time slowly forcing her lips apart, completing the kiss. He held it for a good half moment, feeling her slowly starting to respond. After that, he began kissing her on the neck and then down her front toward her breasts. He had his right hand on her side. He felt the tremble run through her as he took her nipple into his mouth. He worked it with his tongue, feeling it grow hard under his caress. Now her lips had parted slightly and he could hear her breathing increase.

He took her small hand, surprisingly smooth in spite of the work she was forced to do, and put it on his penis. Almost involuntarily she began to stroke him. He could feel desire rising.

She said, ''Please do it. Do it now. I'm so afraid of what I might miss if you don't hurry.''

He wanted to tell her that she wasn't ready yet and he wanted to tell her that he wasn't ready yet, but he guessed that she wanted to practice. He thought he would do the best he could. He got up on his knees and carefully worked his way over her legs, slowly spreading them in the process. Then he leaned down on her and guided himself into her vagina. She was dry and it was difficult to penetrate. At one point, she let out a half-muffled scream and he could tell that it had hurt her. He worked slower, trying to get an arousal, trying to get her juices flowing. Finally, he was in her but still she lay inert making no move to participate. His mouth was next to her ears. He whispered, "Sarah, put your arms around me and raise up and lock your legs around my hips." She did it in a mechanical fashion.

If it had not been so long, he doubted that he could have accomplished his part. As it was, he had to conjure up visions in his mind of Molly Coy and the acrobatic dressmaker back in Denver. But finally, his natural healthy appetite took over and he began to stroke himself into her with greater vigor and deeper thrusts. He could feel her becoming moist as he worked. He took his mouth from her ear and clamped it onto hers, forcing her mouth to open and her tongue to come out. He grasped her tightly with his strong arms and he could feel her arms pulling at his neck. But the good feeling lasted all too short. He had too much pent-up sex in him to have prolonged the pleasure. All of a sudden, he exploded inside her, raised up and let out a moan as he ejaculated. He could feel her rotating her hips trying to help him, but it was just a fleeting thought in the midst of the tumbling myriad of flashing lights and noises that were going on in his head.

Just as suddenly as he had risen to the top, he collapsed, his whole weight going dead on her. He felt her give a sigh as he lay there.

For a long moment, he didn't move. He was conscious that she was kissing his forehead and then his cheeks and then the other parts of his face she could reach. He carefully disengaged himself and rolled off of her onto his side of the bed.

For a long moment, nothing was said. Then she turned her face toward him and whispered softly, "I'm sorry. I thought it would come back."

Longarm turned sideways so that he could reach her face with his hand. He stroked her cheek. He said, "Sarah, it was fine, just fine. Don't think about it. It was wonderful. It was me that was stiff and awkward. It wasn't your fault."

"It's just been so long, it's hard to explain how I feel inside. He might as well have killed me on the outside as killed me inside."

Longarm said, "Honey, I don't know what you expected. You said that you've been out of the saddle for three years or better. You can't expect to just jump on a horse and ride like you used to."

In the light, he could see her biting at her lip. She said, "It's not just the time without, it's the feelings inside me he put there. It's the cruelty, the hate he showed me. I didn't know people could feel like that. He's an evil man, so cruel, so hard." She suddenly turned her face away.

Longarm hitched himself up on the bed until he was leaning against the headboard. He reached over and got himself a cigarillo and lit it. The flame of the match illuminated both of them more clearly than the lamp. In the sudden flash he could see the sadness in her face. He shook the match out and got his cigarillo drawing good. He said, "Sarah, I think that you're going to have to tell me about your Mr. Richard Brown."

She gave a short bark of laughter. "Tell you about Richard Brown? There is no Richard Brown. Only the Richard part is right."

Longarm said, "I didn't think his name was Brown. I don't know if you're going to tell me his last name or not or if you're going to tell me anything about him. I can tell you this, though. Whatever you do tell me dies with me. I would never give you away for all the money in the world or all the tea in China, but I think you're going to have to talk about it. I'm not going to be here that much longer. This place is not going to hold me and I will find that man and I will either kill him or put him so far deep in jail, they're going to have to roll his supper down to him."

Sarah turned her face to look at him. She said, "Oh, if only I could believe that."

Longarm looked at her grimly. He said, "Believe it."

She was silent for a moment and then she said, quite matter of factly, "I hate him." She paused. "I'm thirty years old, and for at least twenty-nine of those years, I never thought I could say that about anyone. But to see me now, you would have a hard time believing that I was once very sweet, very loving, very affectionate." She paused again. Longarm waited for her to go on. "But he changed that in me. I don't mean just the lovemaking. I don't mean that he made me incapable of feeling passion. He made me feel incapable of love. He's turned all of the good feeling inside me into bitterness and hate, and I hate him for that." She turned her head and looked at Longarm. "Can you understand that?"

He said, "I could understand it a whole lot better if you would tell me who we're talking about. I know that's going to require a wagon load of trust on your part, but honey, you're going to have to trust somebody pretty soon. You're as good as dead right now, the life you're living. I may be your ticket out of here. We're both prisoners. I don't see where you can hurt yourself at all. As near as I can figure, you've got nothing to lose. By the way, that makes me have to ask you something. You've told me all this, how miserable your life is. Why haven't you run for it? Why haven't you gotten the hell out of here? Are you being watched night and day?"

She gave a short, bitter laugh. She said, "No, of course not, but what chance would I, a genteel white woman, have in this country? It's twenty-five miles to the border and he practically controls that part of the land. I have no money, no real clothes. I have no shoes to amount to anything, nothing but slippers. How can I get out of here? I don't really know how to ride a horse, so how would I leave? His men would catch me before I had gone ten miles and then they would do what they did once before. They would tie me to a post out in the hot sun and leave me out there for several days until I was almost dead from thirst and hunger.''

Longarm said, ''I see. Well, whoever Mr. Brown is, he's one no-good low-down son of a bitch, but it's up to you if you want to tell me your story—I'd like to hear it. I can only tell you that you can trust me. I can't prove it. By the time I've proven it you'll be out of here.''

When Longarm finished speaking, she was quiet for a moment. She touched her navel with her forefinger, looking down at it. She said, ''I never really thought of it that way.''

''What way?''

''I really have nothing to lose. What I have now is living death. I think I might almost prefer to be dead rather than to go on living like this. The only thing I have to look forward to in the future is more hate, more mistreatment, more humiliation.'' She paused. After a moment, she said, ''His name is Richard Harding.''

The name bounced around in Longarm's head like a rubber ball. It was familiar, yet he couldn't place it. He said, ''Richard Harding. Richard Harding. I know it from someplace.''

''You should. You both work for the federal government.''

It clicked. He said, ''You're not talking about Judge Richard Harding, are you?''

''Yes,'' she said. ''I'm his ex-wife!''

Longarm's mouth literally fell open. He said, ''Do you mean the Richard Harding who is a federal circuit court judge?''

''Yes, and also one of the biggest crooks along the border and perhaps the most vicious man.''

Longarm said, "You're telling me that a federal court judge kidnapped me and is holding me prisoner?"

"Yes. He's also holding me prisoner, too."

It suddenly made sense in a strange sort of way. A federal judge would know, probably better than anyone, the ins and outs of swapping a federal prisoner for a federal deputy marshal. Longarm had no idea how he was going about it, but now the plan didn't seem so crazy.

Chapter 6

Sarah said, "About three years ago, he caught me with another man. It was innocent enough in appearance, but it wasn't so innocent in my heart. I was so starved for love, for affection, for kindness, that I was ready to throw myself at the first man I could interest, but they were all afraid of Judge Harding and with good reason. I was not quite twenty-seven. He was a young lawyer, newly moved to Laredo. We carried on an innocent enough flirtation for a while and then we arranged to meet. Sufficient to say, Richard caught us." Sarah stopped and turned her face away.

Longarm asked, "What did he do?"

"More the question is: What didn't he do? He put me in the cellar of our house and kept me there for two weeks. I later found out he had the young lawyer killed. Then he gave me a choice: He would either kill me or he would send me to this ranch to live out the rest of my days as a scullery maid. You can see the choice I took."

Longarm stared at her. He said, "Sent his own wife here? To live as a scullery maid?"

"Yes, and made certain that everyone in the place treated me like one. Humiliation heaped upon humiliation. I am the lowest form of life on this ranch. I come below the goats. I eat the scraps. I do the dirtiest work. I get the back of anyone's hand who cares to hit me."

"Did Richard ever beat you?"

Sarah laughed without humor. "Beat me? He burned me with his cigar. He soaked me in a bathtub full of ice. He plucked out my eyebrows, he tore my toenails off. Did he ever beat me? I would have begged for a good honest blow."

Longarm said, "Damn. I would never have thought a man could be that mean."

"Oh, he's well beyond mean."

"How does he explain your absence? Surely, a lot of people knew he was married."

She laughed. "Oh, shortly after the incident I was killed on a trip to Monterrey. I forget the exact details but Richard had me declared dead. So for all practical purposes, Sarah Jane Harding, née Thompson, which was my maiden name, no longer exists. My parents were told and a memorial service was held in my hometown in Kentucky. I am dead except I insist on going on living."

Longarm said grimly, "That makes two of us, honey. I promise you this, Sarah Jane, we're both going to come out of this mess alive and well. Mr. Richard Harding will think he's penned up with a dozen rattlesnakes before I am through with him."

She suddenly reached out and clasped his hand. She said eagerly, "Oh, do you really think so? Mr. Long, do you really think there's a chance?"

He looked around at her. "I know there's a chance. I'm going to need your help, though."

She looked distressed. She asked, "How can I help you? I'm just a woman, a watched woman at that."

"Can you get me a gun?"

Her face fell and she made a hoot of humorless laughter. She said, "A gun? I couldn't get myself within half a mile of a gun. Don't you think if I could have laid my hands on a gun by now that I would've taken great pleasure at shooting everyone on this ranch? All these people who have treated me like dirt and slop—these banditos who work for Richard? Don't you think I would have hidden that gun and waited for one of his infrequent visits and then shoved it into him and then pulled the trigger as many times as I could? A gun, God, I would die for a gun. Yes, I would be willing to die if I could get my hands on a gun and use it on him."

Longarm shrugged and said, "Well, I guess that's out." He thought for a moment. "Sarah, how many men are there on this place?"

Sarah said, "Seven."

"Seven?" Longarm was surprised. "He's got seven pistoleros here?"

"Oh, you mean those gunmen like Miguel and Chulo?"

"Yes."

"Oh, there's only one besides them. His name is Martín. He's Miguel's brother. The other four men work around the place, tending the cattle and the horses and the goats."

"How many women?"

She thought for a moment. "There are six grown women. Two or three are Richard's *putas*, his whores. They are young and beautiful. They don't do anything but lie around. The other three, or maybe four, do the work around the house and the cooking for the Mexican men, and then, of course, there's me."

"And you do the scullery work?"

"I do whatever they tell me to do."

Longarm said, "There's no way out of this wing of the house except through that hall door?"

She shook her head. She said, "There are three rooms on this side and each one is just like this one. In fact, I sleep in the one at the other end of the hall. It's not as nice as this one—it's very small. That door leads into the main room of the house. Beyond it, there is an office and a dining room and a big bedroom and then another bedroom and then, of course, the kitchen."

"So this is a pretty big place?"

"Oh, yes."

"Don't they have a place where they store guns? A glass case? A rack on the wall?"

Sarah nodded her head. "Yes, there is a rack where guns are kept in the office—rifles, not pistols—but they are all chained. You would need a key to the lock. I know that I couldn't get one."

Longarm said, "Let's quit thinking about it for a while. I feel so good having you here with me that I feel nearly free. But I do want to say one thing. I'm worried that your husband—"

She broke in quickly to say, "Don't call him that. He's got another wife, in fact. At least that's what he's told me."

"He's remarried with you still alive?"

"You forget that I'm dead."

"Anyway, I'm worried about how fast Richard Harding can proceed. I hadn't counted on him being a federal district judge. That makes him a good deal more dangerous than I thought."

Sarah looked up at him. "I don't know why, but I feel safe with you even though we're both prisoners. Lying here beside you, I don't feel that anything bad could happen to me.''

"I'm not going to let anything bad happen to you. I'm going to get us both out of here as quickly as I can think of a way." Longarm reached out his hand and began to caress her right breast. It was firm and silky smooth with a big hard nipple, but still she stiffened up at his touch. He said, "Here now, what's the matter? I'm just trying to gentle that horse down that you've got to get back up on and ride."

She said, "I can't help it. You must forgive me, it's been so long."

Longarm slid down on the bed and leaned over and kissed her on the corner of the mouth. "Are you willing to take instruction?"

She turned on her side to meet him and said, "Yes. Oh my, yes. I'm willing to learn anything that you want to teach me."

For the next hour they slowly and gently made love. Longarm took great delight in leading her down a path she hadn't walked in so long that it was almost as if she was on virgin ground again. The fact was, she had never been taught very well to begin with. Her husband had been a cruel, selfish lover with no knowledge of how to please a woman. When it was finally over and Sarah had been stirred beyond heights she confessed to Longarm she never even dreamed existed, she told him how different it had been, that she had never thought lovemaking could be so beautiful, so sensual, so gentle. She said, whispering to him, "It was almost like two people sharing a wonderful secret together, a secret that no one else knows about or will ever know about."

After a while, they both drifted off to sleep. Sometime during the night she got up and left the room. She had warned him in advance that she would need to be back in her own room before dawn. She had also warned him that when she came in with his breakfast the next morning she couldn't act any different. She'd said, "I'll be laughing and gay inside, but you won't see it on the outside. I have to act that way so they won't suspect that we are in league together."

"I understand."

"And you'll be thinking of how I can help us escape?"

"You can bet on that," Longarm said.

He woke the next morning with the sun well up. Sarah hadn't brought his breakfast and for that he was grateful. It gave him time to get up and wash his face and brush his teeth and run a razor over his cheeks. He did the best he could with stroking his hands over his hair, but without a brush, he knew it was still a tangled mess.

He hated to put his jeans back on—he had been wearing them for a week—but he wasn't about to walk around in a sheet the rest of the time, so he reluctantly climbed back into the well-worn denim pants.

It was near eight o'clock by his watch when Sarah let herself back into his room. She was wearing the old robe made from blue blanket material. He tried to act nonchalant, as if there was nothing between them, but she immediately came up and kissed him hard on the mouth, probing her tongue into his. He pulled back and glanced down the hall.

He asked, "What's going on? I thought we had to be careful?"

Sarah said, "They are not watching me so closely this morning. They locked the hall door after me—no one followed."

"Are you sure there's no one in those other rooms?"

"Yes, I looked." She nodded her head vigorously. She suddenly began to unbutton her robe.

Longarm said, alarmed, "Wait a minute, Sarah. We can't do that—"

85

But she cut him off. She said, "I've got some clothes for you. They're Richard's. He's not as big as you are, but maybe they'll still fit. I've got some pants and a good white shirt and some clean socks. I even brought you some clean underwear."

He smiled slightly. "I don't wear underwear so I don't need any."

"Hide your old clothes under the bed and maybe they'll never notice. I got colors that are approximately what you had on. Have you thought of any way I can help yet?"

Longarm kissed her lightly. He said, "No, my dear, but I'm thinking."

Then all too soon she was starting toward the door. He stopped her as she began to turn the knob. He said, "Sarah, be careful. *I* can see the difference in you. They'll spot it immediately."

She smiled. "I'm only like this around you. Outside of this door, I'm the same old beaten-down dead Sarah. Don't worry about that. They don't pay any more attention to me than they would one of the goats." With that, she was gone through the door, locking it behind her.

The room door was no problem. The problem was the door to the hall and the problem was how to get through the door to the hall with a weapon in his hand so anyone trying to stop him could be stopped themselves. He needed a weapon; a revolver, a shotgun, a rifle, something that would work at a distance rather than just face-to-face. He couldn't fight a gun with a knife. He sat down to his breakfast. It was ham and eggs and grits and biscuits and coffee. One thing he could say about the jail Judge Harding had set up was that it fed him good.

After he had finished his breakfast, Longarm sat on the side of his bed with a glass of whiskey in hand and a lit cigarillo and thought. He started off thinking about Judge Richard Harding. Now that he was giving it careful examination, digging into the deep recesses of his memory, he found he knew more about the judge than he had first thought. A federal circuit judge such as Harding had great powers within his district—his circuit. It was a federal circuit judge's job to move from town to town and hold trial in different places. Judge Harding, if Longarm's memory served him correctly, had a district that encompassed a good half of the border and most of southeast Texas, almost to San Antonio. It was a lot of power to put into one man's hand, especially if that man was a crook. But he also remembered that Judge Harding was considered a comer. He wasn't particularly old. Longarm thought of him as being somewhere around forty. It was said that he had friends in high places in Washington. He was also rumored to have money. Supposedly, it was family money, but Longarm reckoned that a crooked federal judge could just about get rich by taking a piece of every illegal dollar that crossed the border. He had no doubts that Judge Harding had done just such a thing. And now, along had come this $200,000 payday. Longarm could see how a situation like that would make an evil man like Harding lick his lips.

It worried Longarm, now that he knew about Harding, that the man might be able to effect some sort of a deal faster than could be expected or faster than he could be stopped. Longarm could only speculate on what method Harding might try, but he might convince officials of the federal bank in San Antonio that he could somehow act as a go-between and not only get him, Longarm, back safely but manage to get Earl Combs to divulge where the money was. Of course, he had no intention of doing any such thing. Once he got control of the situation, he would make Combs tell him where the money was, then kill him and then kill Longarm.

Now that he knew who he was dealing with, Longarm gave no thought to Harding's sincere-sounding vows that he had no desire to have the death of a deputy marshal on his hands.

But that was all well and good. Now he knew his enemy a little bit better, but that didn't get him out of the room and out of the house and on a horse on his way to try and stop Harding. How to do that? He looked around the room for the hundredth time trying to think of some way out. All he had, really, was a penknife and eight cartridges. He couldn't see how any of those were going to do him much good, but as he stared at his gun belt hanging over the back of one of the chairs, he looked hard at the cartridges and then looked over at an empty bottle of whiskey that was sitting on the bedside table. A thought slowly began to work itself into his mind. He glanced at the kerosene lantern. For a moment, he let his mind play around with the idea, and then he shook his head, dismissed the thought, and let his mind go blank.

After he had finished smoking his cigarillo and finished his glass of whiskey, he let the thought come back into his mind. He played with it, looking at it from first one angle and then another. It was possible, just barely possible. A long shot, but then that was all he had for ammunition at the time—long shots.

Longarm got up, went over to his gun belt, extracted a cartridge from its loop, and went back and sat on the bed. First, he put the lead slug of the cartridge between his teeth and tried to twist it. Nothing happened except he could feel the strain he was putting on his teeth. Next, he opened his penknife and took the short stubby blade and ran it between the brass casing and the lead slug. Gently, he began trying to work the slug out of the lead casing. It didn't want to come. After he'd tried for a few moments longer, he saw that the attempt was futile and he dropped his knife and the slug on the bed and stared across at the wall. He needed a pair of pliers. He wondered if Sarah could get them for him. He needed several other things too and he thought she could get them.

With his mind still making plans, he got up and took off his old dirty jeans and dropped them on the floor and kicked them under the bed. He took up the pair of Judge Harding's pants; they were the very highest quality corduroy. He sat down on the bed and ran his legs into them and then stood up and pulled them up around his waist. He had to smile. Mr. Harding's pants were about two inches too short for him, and the waist was about two inches too big. It didn't make any difference, however. At least they were clean. He picked up the shirt and put it on. It was high-quality linen. Apparently it was nothing but the best for the Honorable Judge Richard Harding. He stuffed the shirt into his pants and then took his own belt out of his jeans and put it on, cinching it up tight to keep the pants from falling down. After that he put on the clean socks that Sarah had brought and pulled his boots on. He was tired of walking around in his bare feet, and, besides, he never knew when he was going to have kick someone and it was much more effective kicking someone with a boot on than a bare foot.

Now there was nothing he could do but wait for Sarah to come back for his breakfast dishes so that he could ask her if she could get the things he needed. The plan wasn't fully formulated in his mind, but it looked as if he was going to have to adapt it to the situation as it came.

Chapter 7

Sarah said with a frightened look on her face, "Get you a pair of pliers? Custis, I'm not even sure I know what pliers are or where to get them."

He said, "Sarah, everybody has seen a pair of pliers. They're something you grip with, like tongs. You might find them in the blacksmith shop or in the shed or there might be some in the kitchen. You turn a nut on a bolt with them."

She still looked uncertain. "Well, I can try."

"Well, if you can't get those, get me a stronger knife. I'm trying to work the lead heads out of their brass casings. A pair of pliers would work best, but get me whatever you can."

She had her tray loaded with his breakfast dishes. She said, looking him over, half smiling, "I never thought I would like to see those clothes again. They look so much different on you than they did on him."

Longarm said impatiently, "Honey, we're going to have a long time to talk about this sort of thing. Right now, we've got to get out of here. Now, we need a candle and I need you to bring more kerosene than is necessary for the lamp— a good deal more. And I need a whole big double handful of matches. Can you handle that?''

She looked uncertain. She said, ''I think I can do it all except maybe the pliers. It's not that I can't get them in to you, but it's just that I don't know where I'll find them.''

''Invent an excuse.''

She answered, ''They'd never believe I needed a pair of pliers.''

''Well, try, honey, try. Tell them you got a bent bedspring on your bed. Tell them you need to work a nail out of the wall, tell them anything. But don't tell Miguel or Martín or Chulo, tell one of the Mexican women. Just a small pair of pliers.''

She gave him a halfhearted smile and then raised her face for a kiss. He kissed her lightly and then she was gone out the door, shutting it behind her. He could hear the key turning behind her.

Now all he could do was wait. He walked thoughtfully over to the bedside table and picked up the empty whiskey bottle. There was a full one there that had been brought the night before, but it was the empty one, he thought, that would prove much more valuable than any full bottle of whiskey that he had ever seen, and he certainly didn't think he'd ever be making such a remark as that.

The time passed slowly as he expected it would. He was getting restless, getting cabin fever, getting very tired of the white room with the thick walls and the two little bitty windows and the one light. The food was good, that was all he could say about the place—well, the female companionship wasn't bad either—but he preferred to be able to take a long walk after making love to a beautiful woman, to sort of cool down like you would with a racehorse. You couldn't exactly cool down in a room fifteen by eighteen feet.

But slowly the minutes crept by and turned into hours and the hours stacked up enough until it was one o'clock and he could hear her unlocking the door. The next thing he knew, she was through it in a rush, pushing it nearly shut behind her with her foot. She was wearing the bulky blanket robe. She whispered. "Quick! Reach under my robe. There's a sack there tied with string. Get it out and throw it up under the bed. It's got everything in it."

He moved quickly, running his hand up underneath until he felt the cloth sack tied with string. He whipped out his penknife and cut it quickly and slung the bag under the bed. He stood up while she was busy setting his dishes out on the table. Just as he was able to straighten up, the door was pushed slightly open and Chulo stood there, his white teeth flashing, gleaming in his dark face.

"Ah, here is the lovebirds. No? Hey, señor, how you like this one? She look like a cow, don't you think?"

Longarm sat down on the bed. He said, "I don't know what you're talking about."

Chulo said, "Hey, we send you this woman. Maybe if you don't like her, we don't send her no more."

Longarm said, "You're not being much of a gentleman, Chulo. Why are you trying to embarrass this woman?"

"Hey, this ain't no woman. This just some ol' rag that get cast off, just a stray dog."

Sarah had finished unloading her dishes on Longarm's table. She turned and hurried past Chulo. As she went by, he slapped her on the rear end with the back of his hand, a slap that was harder than necessary.

Longarm felt his jaw muscles tighten. He said, "Hey, don't be bruising the goods. Do you mind?"

Chulo laughed loudly. He said, "Ho, ho. Maybe you in love, huh, señor? You want to marry this cow? This stray dog we got here? This bitch? Maybe your dick rot off, you fuck her again.'' With that, still laughing, he turned on his heels, pulled the door shut behind him, and locked it.

It had unsettled Longarm slightly that the man had come after Sarah. It had not been part of his plan. He had understood why she wanted him to move quickly. He had hoped for more time to talk to her; now he was going to have to wing it, play it by ear. It could get very dangerous with her not knowing what he was going to do. Hopefully, she would be back in a couple of hours to gather up his dishes as she normally did. The pistoleros had not been accompanying her. All he could do was hope that Chulo's visit had been casual, not planned. Perhaps he had just wanted to look in on the star boarder and see how he was doing. It was very important that he have time to explain to her what had to happen for them to reach freedom. Hope was the one commodity that he had the most of. He had eight cartridges, an empty whiskey bottle, a candle, a bunch of matches, some kerosene, a woman who was ignorant of his plans, and overlaying all of that was a big mess of hope. He smiled to himself and shook his head. Well, it didn't much matter. He had to proceed with his part and he had plenty to do. He ducked under the bed, got the sack up, and opened it. There was a small pair of pliers, a lot of matches with big phosphorus heads, and a candle. There was no extra kerosene and that worried him. But he had to get to work just as if he knew what he was doing. He found a newspaper, one of the two-week-old ones that they had brought him. He spread a single sheet out on the bed and then took his knife and began working on the matches. He was shaving the phosphorus heads off the wood. He figured he had about a hundred matches, it was a slow and tedious job but he needed those match heads. He had been careful to hide the rest of his equipment under the bed so if the door was suddenly opened by the wrong party, he'd be able to cover up his work simply by laying another sheet of newspaper on top of what he was doing.

It took him about forty-five minutes, but he finally ended up with a nice pile of yellow and white phosphorous match heads. Now with his fingers, he began to crumble them into a substance like cornmeal. When that was done, he very carefully folded the paper over about an inch from the edge. With that creased, he took his knife and slowly made a long line of the crumbled match heads along the length of the newspaper. He was making a fuse. When the crumbled phosphorus was evenly stretched the length of the paper, he carefully cut along a line even with the edge he had turned over. Then, being careful not to lose any of the precious ignitable material, he rolled the narrow piece of newspaper into a single thin straw. To keep the contents in place, he twisted it at one-inch intervals, being careful to twist each end closed first. The result was a fuse about two and a half feet long and about the thickness of a big hay straw. He put the fuse under the bed and then got his cartridges and the pliers. Using another piece of newspaper, he gripped the lead head of each cartridge and slowly twisted the slug loose from the casing. Then with the point of his knife, he removed the thin wad that stood between the powder and the slug. When that was done, he poured the powder carefully onto the newspaper. He breathed very shallowly. He couldn't afford to lose a single speck of it.

It took an hour to carefully get every bit of powder out of the eight cartridges. After that, he got the empty whiskey bottle and, making a funnel out of the newspaper, poured the powder carefully into the bottle. It made a disappointingly small amount but it was going to have to do. He methodically dropped all eight brass casings and all eight lead slugs into the bottle. He looked longingly at the lamp. It was only half full. He needed the bottle full. The candle still remained to be used, but he couldn't use it or insert his fuse until, or if, he could get some more kerosene. Once again, hope was the only horse he had to ride. He carefully hid the bottle behind the bed and then sat down to wait.

It was almost three o'clock by his watch before a key turned in the door and it opened. Sarah was there and he saw that she was unaccompanied. To his relief he saw that, along with his tray, she was carrying a small tin bucket with a spout on it. He could almost smell the kerosene.

He said, "Hurry, Sarah, hurry! Shut the door."

She rushed forward holding out the can of kerosene. He unscrewed the cap off the spout, found his whiskey bottle, poured it almost full. She stood by, watching in wonder. He said, "You better get to picking up those dishes or they'll wonder why you're so long."

"Right," she said.

Longarm finished with the kerosene, screwed the cap back on the spout, and then carefully hid his whiskey bottle now full of kerosene back behind the bed. Now came the part that was the most important.

He went up to Sarah, first glancing down the hallway to make sure no one was near. He said, "Honey, you've got to do something and you've got to bring it off. There's no two ways about it."

She looked up at him, frightened. She asked, "What?"

"You've got to get one of the three pistoleros to come back with you and they have to be wearing a gun."

She said, "How do I do that?"

"I don't know. Maybe tell them I tried to take the key away from you, or maybe that I ran into the hall. Tell them you're afraid of me, tell them anything. Tell them that I want to see them, that I've got some information for them. Tell them anything, but get one of them to come with you."

She swallowed. "Can you tell me what's going to happen?"

"You saw that whiskey bottle?"

She nodded. He said, "If things go right, that whiskey bottle is going to get us a pistol, a revolver, a gun, a way out of here."

She looked uncertain. "How is that going to happen?"

"I want you to do exactly what I tell you," he said. "Don't worry about what's going to happen. If you know what's going to happen, you'll worry and you'll give it away. You'll be too nervous, so I won't tell you."

Her voice broke a little as she said, "All right."

He said, "When you come in with my supper, come straight to the table. I will be on the other side of the bed. Let out a shriek, yell, drop the tray, and throw yourself to the floor as far away from the door as you can. Try to edge yourself under the bed."

She looked at him in wonder. "Why would I want to do that?"

"You can't ask me any questions. Just do it."

Her eyes searched his face. "Well, if you say so, but what if more than one of them comes?"

"Try to just get one, but if more than one of them comes, I'll have to handle it as it is. Just do what I tell you. You come in first, drop your tray at the table, dive under the bed. That's all. And you yell, scream as loud as you can. Make as much commotion as you can."

She let out a long shuddering sigh. She said, "Custis, I'm not used to this sort of thing. I'm not brave like you are. I'm not sure I can do it."

He reached out and softly stroked her hair. He said, "Honey, it's not that I'm brave. I'm desperate and I think you are, too. Now, you can do this. Don't you worry. You only have to do that small part. If you get one of those pistoleros to that door, I'll take over from there.''

She smiled bravely and said, "Yes, I'll do my best. I don't know what I'll say, but I'll get one of them here.''

He leaned down and kissed her. She put her arms around his neck and kissed him back, hard. Then he let her go and she picked up the tray and walked to the door. She looked back at him, wistfully.

He said, "It won't be long."

She said with a faint smile, "I was sort of looking forward to tonight."

"Tonight ain't necessarily out. It just might be somewhere else."

She pulled the door to behind her and locked it. He sat down on the bed. Now came the hardest part of all. The wait to see if she could successfully return with one of the pistoleros. If she couldn't, then all of his planning would have been in vain.

It was about time to put the final touches on his bomb, if it could be called that. He got the whiskey bottle out and held it up. It was above the neck of the bottle with kerosene and the powder lay about half an inch thick at the bottom, though some of it was floating around near the top. He took the candle she had brought him and got his penknife out. The idea was to get the fuse inserted into the bottle and then plug it with a solid piece of wax and then drip more wax on that to seal it tight. He cut a piece about an inch long off the bottom of the candle with his pocketknife. He tried it in the mouth of the bottle, but it was too big. He carefully wittled it down, making it taper toward the end he was going to shove into the bottle. After several tries, he had it so the piece of wax would slide down snugly into the mouth of the bottle. After that, he took his knife and very carefully cut a small channel along the length of the candle cork. That was to accommodate the fuse. Being careful not to lose any of the ground-up match heads, he stuck the fuse down until it just touched the kerosene and began to wick up some of the flammable liquid. Then he took the candle stopper, positioning the little vee he'd cut into the wax over the fuse and shoved it down hard. If his plans went as they should, the wax should allow the fuse fire to pass through, igniting the kerosene, which would ignite the powder and explode the whole bottle. Slugs and brass casings and glass would fly every which way and there would be with a lot of smoke, noise, and confusion.

That was if it worked.

He struck a match and lit the rest of the candle where the wick was sticking out. Holding it carefully away so as not to set the bomb off too soon, he began to drip the melted wax around the fuse hole and all around the sides where the candle stopper met with the glass of the bottle. He did it slowly and carefully, and when he was through he was certain that the bomb, at least, was airtight, which was necessary to create an explosion. He held it up to the light and looked at it carefully. It looked lethal enough with the eight lead slugs and the eight brass casings and the kerosene and the powder, but he hadn't the slightest idea in the world if it would work. Maybe it would be nothing but a loud fizzle, but even if it just smoked a little, it might give him the chance, the brief instant he needed, to get his hands on a gun.

There was nothing more he could do. He walked over to the door and placed the bomb against the wall about a foot from the doorway entrance. The fuse hung down about two feet and, because the paper was stiff, it did not touch the floor but just drooped over slightly. The idea was that he was going to light the fuse and hope that it burned fast enough to catch whichever pistolero came in and explode before the man could see the danger. The problem was that he had no idea how fast the fuse was going to burn. It should burn very quickly. Of course, if it burned too quickly, it wouldn't allow him to get to safety on the other side of the bed or Sarah to get to safety underneath the bed. But he would simply have to guess. He didn't have another fuse to test and wasn't likely to get one. It was the kind of experiment that would have to work on the first try.

Now time hung heavy on his hands. He paced about the room, looked at himself in the mirror, thought about shaving, discarded the idea, put his hat on, looked in the mirror again, had a drink, and finally sat down on the bed with one of the two-week-old newspapers to see what had been happening in San Antonio.

It got to be four o'clock by his watch and then five, and finally, six. All he could think about was how intricate, how delicate, how very improbable his plan was. It depended on too many things that were out of his control. He didn't like it. He didn't like it at all. He thought that maybe the best thing to do would be to rush whoever was at the door—throw a picture at him or whatever. Anything but this infernal weapon that he had created in an empty whiskey bottle.

But then it was probably all for naught anyway. Most likely Sarah wouldn't succeed in getting one of the pistoleros to come back with her. If she complained he was trying to get the keys away from her, they would probably just laugh. It wouldn't make any difference to them if he got out of his particular cell. He wouldn't make it through the hall door anyway.

Finally he tried to put all thoughts out of his head. Whatever was going to happen would. He'd at least done his best and he couldn't do any more. After that, he settled down to wait with an easy mind.

When the time came, he was almost caught off guard. As the key was turned in the doorway, he was on the wrong side of the bed without any matches in his hand. He instantly jumped up from the bed, rushed forward just as the door began to open, and threw himself up against the wall next to the bottle.

At that instant, Sarah threw the door wide and came in. Longarm had struck a match that was burning in his hand. He could see the outline of someone's boots. He leaned down and lit the fuse and in two steps was on the other side of the bed. Miguel was in the doorway, the older of the two pistoleros who had first taken him prisoner. He saw the Mexican glance at him, saw the surprised look on his face, and then he saw Sarah trip, throw the tray, and then heard her scream. Longarm was watching Miguel's face. He saw the Mexican advance toward the woman. He saw the man take two steps inside the room. Longarm yelled "Hey!" at Miguel.

The Mexican whipped his head toward Longarm. His hand went toward his holster. Longarm went limp and let himself fall below the bed. Out of the corner of his eye, as he had fallen, he had seen that the fuse was racing toward the bottle. After that, he didn't know what had happened. There was a sudden boom and the room was full of whizzing objects and full of noise.

Longarm was on his feet in an instant. He raced around the bed, looking for Miguel in the white smoke that filled the room. The pistolero was down on the floor. Longarm dove toward him, but as he grabbed the man, he realized there was no rush. The smoke was lifting and he could see blood coming from several places in the man's abdomen and chest.

Longarm turned his head and looked for Sarah. He could see her, half under the bed. She glanced back at him as if to say she was all right. He was reaching for Miguel's pistol that lay on the floor beside him when he heard the sound of the lock being turned in the hall door. He grabbed the pistol, cocking it as he rose. He could see the door beginning to open. He yelled for Sarah to stay down and then he took one, two, three steps and dove forward, sliding down the slick hard tiles as Chulo came around the end of the open door. He had his pistol in his hand as Longarm fired off a snap shot at him. He saw the slug take the Mexican in the right shoulder, knocking him backward and away from the door. He didn't go down. He was struggling to bring his gun up. Longarm cocked his pistol and fired again. This time, the bullet took the Mexican in the middle of his chest, knocking him backward and flat on his back. Longarm didn't pause. There would be more coming through the door any second. He jumped up. Sarah was still down but she was facing the door.

He yelled at her, "Come on! Come on! Get up." He reached down, grabbed her by the hand and started running toward the door at the end of the hallway.

She said, "I'm afraid . . . the noise scared me."

Longarm said, "There's a lot more waiting out there that scares me. Now come on!"

He got to the door, holding Sarah behind him, and peeked around the edge. He could see into a big room. He motioned with his hand for her to get the gun that lay beside Chulo. He said, "Give me that pistol."

She said, "Is he dead?"

"Yes, he's dead. Damn it, hurry up."

As he looked, Longarm saw a man he didn't recognize come into the room carrying a shotgun. He was perhaps thirty feet away, too far to risk a pistol shot, and he wasn't going to burst into the room. Not against a scatter gun.

The Mexican looked uncertain. He looked first to the right and then to the left and then he glanced across at the door. He didn't seem to have heard the shots, Longarm thought, or he would be coming immediately toward the hall door.

He felt, rather than saw, Sarah handing him the revolver. He took it in his left hand and shoved it into his belt. He had seen, taking a very quick look, that there were only two cartridges left in the pistol he had taken from Miguel and he hoped there were six in Chulo's revolver.

He said to Sarah, "I've got to get that guy in there, the one with the shotgun. He may be the last of the banditos, I don't know."

She said, "Stoop down and let me look."

He was surprised at how calm she sounded. At first, he thought she was going to become hysterical. She was doing well, he thought.

"Yes, that's Martín. He's the mean one."

"Honey, right now, they're all mean ones. Look, right now, I've got to figure out how to get him closer. He's too far away."

They were both peering around the edge of the door. Longarm had pushed the door almost shut as he had walked down after he had shot Chulo. He was watching the man she called Martín, who was a heavyset man probably somewhere in his forties. The man had a bushy mustache and he was wearing a traditional sombrero. The room was large and toward the back was a dining area with several windows. Martín looked uncertain. Longarm guessed that he had heard the noise but hadn't been able to place it. He had glanced toward the hall door several times, but he had made no move in their direction. Now he went to the part of the room where the dining table stood and looked out the windows. For a second, Longarm thought of trying to slip out and get close enough to either have a shot at him or cover him to make him drop the gun. The danger to Longarm was that the man might go outside or disappear into another room. If that happened, Longarm would not only lose track of the man and his shotgun, but he would also lose the very important element of surprise. He drew back from the door a foot or so, pushing Sarah back. He whispered to her, "I want you to scream."

She said, "What?"

"I want you to scream as loud as you can and yell for help." He motioned with his hand past the door toward the room where he had been held prisoner. "Go halfway down the hall and yell from there so he will think it's coming from my room."

She said, "Isn't that dangerous?"

"Honey," he said. "Let me worry about the danger part. Now, go and scream."

As she slipped past him, he slowly rose to his feet, keeping an eye peering just around the door. He was bareheaded, his hat back in the bedroom. He glanced at Sarah. She had walked a few paces past him and stopped in the hallway facing him. He nodded his head. She let out a tentative scream. He raised his hand upward, urgently. She screamed louder, then louder still. He watched the man suddenly whirl around and start back into the main living room. Sarah began yelling for help. The man fixed his eyes on the door and came walking rapidly forward, his shotgun at the ready but not pointed at anything. Longarm let him come on. Let him get to twenty feet away, then fifteen feet. At ten feet, he threw the door open and stepped into the opening. As he did, Martín stopped dead and tried to swing the shotgun up. Longarm extended his arm and, before the shotgun came level, he fired. He saw the slug catch the man below the throat latch. The man was heavyset and the bullet did not knock him down. He staggered backward, firing one barrel of the double-barrel shotgun into the ceiling. Longarm cocked the revolver and shot him again, this time a little lower in the chest. The man went down, heavily, falling full out, his head thudding against the tile floor. With the echo of his own shots and the shotgun blast still ringing in the air, Longarm whirled. It was time to hurry. By now, surely everyone outside would have been alerted. He could only hope that the guy who worked the vegetable garden or the ones who worked the cattle and the horses didn't intend to get brave or try anything foolish.

He rushed back down the hall, past Sarah, and ran into the room where he had been kept prisoner. He grabbed his hat and jammed it on his head and then went over to Miguel's body and looked for any extra cartridges. There were none. He dropped the pistol, now useless, beside the body and went running back down the hall, grabbing Sarah by the hand. He stopped to take a look at Chulo to see if he had been carrying any extra cartridges. His gun belt was bare. With that, still tugging Sarah along behind him, he swept through the door at the end of the hallway and out into the big living area of the hacienda. Sarah gave a little start when she saw the dead man lying on the floor. She said, ''Oh my! Oh my!''

Longarm stopped only long enough to scoop up the shotgun in one hand and feel in Martín's shirt pocket with the other. He found two shells. He jammed them in his pocket and then began running with Sarah toward the back of the house.

They went through the kitchen. A fat Mexican woman was cowering behind a table, looking frightened. Longarm paid her no attention. Holding the shotgun with his left hand, he threw the back door open and dove out to land on the ground beyond the steps. There was no one in sight. He motioned for Sarah to join him. He walked around to the back of the house. Standing there were two horses already saddled. They didn't look like much. He suspected they were being used by the vaqueros working the cattle. But they were a ticket out of the place.

He turned to Sarah. He said, "Quick! Let's mount up. We've got to get out of here." He had already untied the horse he was going to ride when he became aware that she was just standing there. "What's the matter? Hurry, we don't have much time."

She said, "I can't ride."

Chapter 8

For a second he stared at her, dumbfounded. He didn't believe he had ever heard anyone say that before. He asked, "What do you mean you can't ride? Are you hurt?"

Looking down at her hands, she said, "No, I've just never learned how to ride except one way, and that only a little."

"What way?"

"Sidesaddle. That's how ladies ride in Kentucky."

He swore for half a second. Then he said, "Well, then you're fixing to learn in an awful hurry."

She said, "How?"

He was already hurrying toward her. "By doing." As quickly as he could, he pulled the stirrup leather up on each side of the saddle so that the stirrups were pulled up about ten inches to a foot. With her standing beside him, he had become aware of how small she was. He didn't know why he hadn't noticed it in the room before, but she couldn't have been more than five foot two or three.

He threw the reins of the horse she was going to ride back

up and then tied them behind the saddle horn. There was a *riata*, a rope on her saddle. He quickly untied it and made a loop around the horse's neck and then pitched the rest of the rope across the saddle of the horse he was going to ride. Before she could say anything, he grasped her around the waist and lifted her up into the saddle. Her dress ballooned around her waist. She tried, girlishly shy, to push it back down. She said, "Oh my! Oh my!"

He said, "Ain't no time to be bashful now, missy."

"But it's so high up here."

"All you've got to do is hold on."

Longarm went around to his own horse and threw the reins over the saddle horn. As he started to mount, he remembered the shotgun that he had leaned against the hitching post. He picked it up with his left hand and stepped up into the saddle, and as he did so, he caught movement out of the corner of his eye. A man had come around the end of the small barn and was standing there. He looked relatively harmless, a little chubby, but he had a pitchfork in his hand. Longarm wheeled his horse around and started toward the man. The man disappeared quickly back into the barn. Longarm looked around for a long moment, sweeping the horizon. Finally, he took a dally around his saddle horn of the rope that he was going to lead Sarah's horse with, then turned his own horse out away from the hitching post and began to guide the animal away from the back of the house. He kept the shotgun at the ready. Sarah's horse came around, leading about four feet behind his mount.

Longarm constantly switched his eyes from the house on his left to the barns and the outbuildings behind him. There was no sign of anyone. As he went by the side of the house he could see the cook's face in the window. She was the only person he saw. He looked back as they cleared the house. About two hundred yards away, he saw a man walking in from a pasture. He didn't seem to be in any hurry.

But Longarm was in a hurry. There was a road leading away from the ranch house but he didn't recall them traveling very far on smooth ground after they had quit the rough country on the way in.

He looked back at Sarah. She was gripping the saddle horn with both hands, looking terrified. He could see with some satisfaction that she had her feet correctly placed in the stirrups and that the stirrups were short enough. He said, "Put some of your weight on your feet in the stirrups. That way, you won't bounce so much. If you keep your weight off the saddle, you won't feel the horse's back. We've got to move along, now. Do you have any idea where there is a road that leads toward the border?"

She looked vaguely around. She said, her voice breaking a little with the motion of the horse, "I only came out here once before I was exiled by Richard. We came out here in a carriage so I don't remember it too well. I have a vague memory of a road somewhere, but I don't know where it is."

Longarm looked toward the west. The sun was already hanging low in the sky. He figured there was no more than an hour and a half, perhaps two hours, of daylight left. He hated to cross country with no idea of where they were headed, but he felt convinced that if they headed northeast, they would strike the Monterrey to Nuevo Laredo road. He thought that's what they had done when they had ridden out. The path they were riding on now went due east. He expected that it too would hit the road, but he calculated it was the long way. He said, "Sarah, we have really got to hurry so I'm going to cut across country. You hold on as best as you can. That's all you have to do. Just hold on to that saddle horn and keep going."

Sarah gave him a brave smile. "I'll try."

Longarm winked at her. "You're doing fine. By the way,

I never did tell you what a good job you did getting me that stuff and then getting Miguel to come to the room. What did you tell him anyway?''

She smiled at Longarm, looking pleased with herself. ''I knew he loved to gamble so I told him you had some money and that you were bored and wanted to play cards for money.''

Longarm laughed. He said, ''That was good thinking.''

''Oh, but it was frightening.'' She shook her head in distress.

''You mean the bomb?'' he asked.

She said, ''Especially that.'' She shuddered. ''It was the first time I have ever seen anyone killed.'' She looked over at Longarm. ''What does it feel like to kill someone?''

He turned his face forward. He said, ''It ain't something you can describe and it really ain't something that ought to be described. Trust me, there ain't no pleasure to it, no matter who the hombre is.''

''I think Richard likes it,'' she said.

''Why?''

''Because he's told me about having people killed and he giggles.''

''Giggles?''

''Yes, like a schoolgirl.''

Longarm whistled. He said, ''Judge Harding is quite a fellow, isn't he?''

She said with a tone in her voice he couldn't quite place, ''If you only knew. Oh, how blind I was. He was so handsome, so dashing, so charming.''

''How long did that last?''

''It seemed like one day. As soon as we got to the border, he changed instantly.''

''What did he want with you, then, if he was going to be cruel to you?'' asked Longarm.

109

She smiled bleakly. "I used to be pretty—very pretty. I used to be the belle of the ball. He liked to show me off, but that was all, show me off."

Longarm said, "I see." He didn't say any more.

They had now come to a place where he decided to turn toward the northeast and head off into the rough country. The going wasn't so bad for the first mile as they wove in and out of mesquite thickets and greasewood bushes, but before long the terrain started to descend and they were going across cuts and washouts and hummocks. He was keeping the horses going at as fast a walk as he thought they could manage. Because the rope kept getting tangled in the bushes, he had brought Sarah's horse right up alongside his so that her horse's head was slightly ahead of his knee on his right side. He was beginning to wonder about the wisdom of cutting across country as he was. They probably would have made better time if they had stayed on the path, but he didn't know if the path would lead to the main road.

From time to time, he would glance around at Sarah. She was having a rough time of it. Her face was red and she was sweating and he could see the whiteness of her knuckles as she tried to choke the saddle horn to death. So far, she'd made no complaint, but after about an hour of the rough going, she said, "Please, can't we stop and rest?"

Longarm shook his head and didn't bother to look back at her. He said, "We can't, Sarah. We've got to hurry."

"But no one will be chasing us from the ranch," she said.

Longarm said grimly, "That's not why I'm hurrying. I'm hurrying because I want to catch your husband before he gets away with a very rich crime."

She said, "But I can't go on. I'm sore. I'm hurting."

"Honey, you're going to be a lot sorer before we get to town."

It was not Sarah that Longarm was the most worried about,

it was the horses. Over the bad ground, it would be no trick at all for one of the horses to step wrong and break a leg or go lame, and they were in the wrong place and in the wrong part of the country to have anything go wrong with their transportation. He had no choice, however, but to press along as fast as he could. Harding already had too big a start. Longarm had to get word to Billy Vail and somehow stop the man. He didn't know how he was going to go about it, not yet anyway, but he figured he had several more hours to think about it.

They dragged on as night began to fall. Dusk came like a kind of mist. There were dark clouds in the sky, and far off toward the east, Longarm could see dark thunderclouds and little flickers of lightning. That, he thought, was all they needed—a hell of a thunderstorm to make the hard clay ground slick and slippery. That would finish off the horses for sure and they had been none too good to start with.

From behind him, Sarah asked timidly, "Is it going to rain?"

He glanced back at her. She looked bedraggled and tired and as if she wished desperately she was someplace else, but she had been good so far. She hadn't spoken for almost an hour. All he had heard out of her had been soft suppressed moans every now and then. He could imagine that she was good and sore. If you weren't used to riding astride a horse, just an easy walk along a smooth path could be a chore, much less riding on a stiff-legged misgaited pony over rough, harsh ground where you're cutting back and forth almost constantly and you're not used to the motion of the saddle.

Longarm eyed the clouds and said, "I sure hope it doesn't. Not until we get to some level ground. If we get caught on one of these slopes in a downpour, we got trouble."

She said, "I'm so thirsty, I almost don't care."

"Why didn't you mention you needed water?"

"I didn't know we had any," she said.

There was a big gallon canteen hanging off his saddle horn. He hadn't tested the water in it, but he supposed somebody had. He got it up and unscrewed the top and took a drink. It was warm and brackish but it was wet. He handed it back to her, watching while she tilted the canteen up to her mouth and then made a face as she drank. When she lowered the canteen, she said, "Oh, that tastes awful."

Longarm said, "Well, sometimes, when you're thirsty enough, even mud will do the chore."

She handed him back the canteen and he took another drink and screwed the top back on and looped the strap of the canteen back over his saddle horn. What he wished he hadn't forgotten was the full bottle of whiskey that had been standing on the bedside table when he had rushed back into the room to get his hat and his gun belt. But in the rush, he simply had overlooked it and he hadn't thought of either food or drink. He had assumed that time was more important and that they would make Laredo soon enough to get food and drink before they expired. As it was, he wasn't so sure. It was becoming increasingly difficult to pick his way through the thick brush and the rough ground, encumbered as he was by having the other horse right up next to his. He had to look for openings in the terrain that would accommodate two horses side by side.

He was also beginning to worry about the condition of the two ranch ponies. They were holding up fairly well so far, but he could hear them both heave for breath if they had to scramble up a washout or if they were struggling to keep from sliding down a sharp incline. He feared neither one of them would ever see ten years old again and had never had the best of care. People in Mexico, Longarm always thought, seemed to consider a horse a disposable animal. Feed him just enough to keep him alive, use him as hard as you could, and then when he died, step off and remove your saddle and get another one.

It had come fair dark now. Fortunately, the moon was coming up and it was a good three-quarter moon, enough to cast some helpful light. But it was coming up in the corner of the sky where the dark clouds still hovered. As it rose it would be obscured by the clouds. He could only hope the storm was working its way toward the east and not heading toward them.

Sarah said, "How are you going to catch Richard?"

Longarm looked back at her. He said, "You didn't call him your husband, you never do. You always call him Richard."

She shrugged. She said, "I'm supposed to be dead, remember? I don't think of him as my husband anymore. As a matter of fact, I haven't thought of him as my husband for a long, long time, even before he sent me to exile at his stolen cattle ranch."

Longarm gave her a hard look. "Is that what he has that place for?"

"I think so. I don't know. He does some funny things with the customs people. He used to get drunk and brag about what they were doing."

Longarm nodded. He said, "Ah, that's where he got the papers on the horse."

She asked, "What papers? What horse?"

Longarm shook his head. "It doesn't matter."

"What are you going to catch him for? What crime are you going to charge him with?" she said.

Longarm said, "Well, I'd like to stop him from committing another one. But as it stands now, I've got enough on him to put him away for a good long time, including what he's done to you. Then there's bigamy and the business of taking a United States deputy marshal hostage. Oh, I'd say the young man has quite a few discards in his pile that he's going to have to answer for, but right now, my main interest is to stop him in his latest scheme. I think a man's life might well be in jeopardy, but more than that, I fear that there might be enough cash money involved that it would cause him to try and break from this country and escape abroad either to South America or someplace in Europe, England or such."

She said, "You know, it's funny. I don't hate Richard. I guess I should. I should hope that you hold him down and stick lit cigarettes to him or cigars as he did to me several times. But I don't. That's funny, isn't it?"

Longarm said, "No, some folks are just of a more forgiving nature, I guess."

They didn't talk any more for a while. The terrain was beginning to ease and Longarm took hope as the country grew tamer. They were almost onto prairie. With the exception of the mesquite and post oak and the greasewood bushes, it would have been easy going. Now he pressed on more toward the north. One advantage he had about coming in at night was that he would be able to see the lights of Nuevo Laredo and Laredo from quite a distance off. That, however, was about the only advantage he could see. Once, after they had been riding on the level prairie for half an hour, his horse suddenly stumbled, and for one sickening moment, Longarm thought he was going down, but then he took three quick steps and righted himself. For a few strides after that, he limped and Longarm thought he had injured a cannon bone in his right front leg. He held his breath for another four or five minutes until the horse settled back into a gait.

Longarm got out his watch and struck a match to see the time. It was a quarter of nine. He wasn't sure at what time they had left the ranch. He guessed it was somewhere around six. He had estimated it was about a four-hour trip to Nuevo

Laredo. That was based on the time they had taken when they had brought him out, but that had been four men on good horses who knew the country. Now they were one man and one woman on two sorry horses and neither one of them knew the country.

Then, at long last, he saw a faint glow on the horizon. If he was correct in his reckoning, they should be striking the Monterrey Road at any time. It was difficult to tell how far away the lights were; it depended on how clear the air was. Sometimes, in the desert, you could see something that looked a mile or two away and it would turn out to be fifty miles. He knew, of course, that the lights of Laredo weren't that far away, but right then, he would have liked for them to have been numbered in yards rather than miles.

In another five minutes, they struck the Monterrey Road and turned left and headed toward the glow of the towns. Sarah said faintly, "Is it much farther? I don't know how much longer I can hold on."

He pulled her horse up level with his. He said, "Take it easy, Sarah. We've got it made now, I think."

But, almost as he said it, Sarah's horse gave a sigh and began to quiver. Longarm could feel him—his leg was pressed up against the shoulder of the horse—and he knew the animal was foundering. As quick as he could, he stopped both animals and jumped from his own horse. He ran around to Sarah's horse, pulling out his penknife as he did. There was one remedy that old ranchers had said would work sometimes. He jammed the blade of his knife into the horse's neck. Blood gushed forth for a moment and then slowed to a trickle. Little by little, the trembling slowed and the animal seemed to start breathing better. In a frightened voice, Sarah said, "What's wrong? Why did you stick the knife in him?"

"It's supposed to cool their blood off. They get overheated

and founder and then die. We may have saved him, I don't know.''

He decided to walk and lead both animals for a ways. He was not particularly fond of walking in high-heeled boots, but right then, he was so scared that the horse would drop dead on him, he didn't know what to do. He didn't think the animal he was riding could carry double even if that double was someone as light as Sarah.

He walked for thirty minutes, giving both horses a rest as they shambled along. Finally, his feet couldn't take it any longer and he remounted. They rode on.

The lights were much closer now. He could almost make out the dim outline of buildings. He guessed they were no more than a mile or two from the outskirts of Nuevo Laredo. Off to his left, he thought he could see the white house where he had been taken prisoner. It was a strange feeling to see that place after so long. It was dark and looked uninhabited, but he felt sure it was the same place.

He nursed them in, reaching Nuevo Laredo, going slowly through the streets, drawing stares. He supposed Sarah looked odd sitting atop the big long-legged Mexican pony with her shortened stirrups and her dress ballooned up around her hips. She had smoothed it down as best as she could, but he knew she still felt awkward and embarrassed. Normally, he would have walked around the town, but he couldn't trust the two horses so he took the straightest line he could.

They passed over customs at the International Bridge and kept going. It was another half mile to the best hotel on the border. A big square concrete and brick building that had been welcoming travelers ever since Longarm had been on the border. He didn't know if he had been recognized by any one in U.S. customs or not. He did know from what Sarah had said that Richard Harding had done criminal business with U.S. customs inspectors, but he believed they knew

116

nothing about Harding's plans for Earl Combs and his $200,000.

He pulled up in front of the hotel and eased tiredly out of the saddle. Before he helped Sarah down, he pulled the shotgun out of the boot and crooked it over his arm. Then he reached up, grasped Sarah under the shoulders and lifted her off the mount. She could barely stand. He had to walk her back and forth before she could regain her legs. Finally, he said, "Are you ready to go in and get a bath and a good meal and whatever clean clothes they can scare up for you?"

She looked up at him, her eyes almost glazed over. She said, "Oh my, oh my, oh my."

He said, "From the look of things, I've got to get us separate rooms in here. Do you understand?"

She nodded. "I suppose so." She suddenly gripped his arm very hard. "But I'm afraid. Richard has friends in this town."

Longarm said grimly, "So do I."

Chapter 9

The owner of the hotel was an old acquaintance. His name was Martin Silver and he had been around the border long enough to have given favors and taken favors and kept secrets and he had learned not to ask too many questions. Once he was summoned by the desk clerk, things moved rapidly. Longarm got them adjoining rooms on the second floor. He told Sarah truthfully that the hotel was known for its strong doors and reliable locks. He didn't think there was a chance that she would be in any danger during the time he would have to be gone, but she looked like a lady who needed all the reassurance she could get. He got her settled in her room. A bath had been arranged for her and Martin Silver had assured Longarm that he would find some woman's clothes for the lady even if he had to send home to his own house. The kitchen was still operating and a meal would be sent up for both of them, but Longarm stopped him at that point and asked that his be held. He said, ''Martin, I've got important business that's got to be taken care of. Now, I'm going to leave this lady in your care and I'm going to assume that she will be just fine when I get back from some business that I need to tend to."

Martin Silver was a distinguished-looking gentleman in his early fifties, but Longarm knew there was rawhide under the gentlemanly manners and dress. Silver said, "Custis, you can be sure that the hospitality of the house also extends to the lady's safety. I will see to that."

Longarm smiled. "That's good enough for me, Martin."

When the hotel owner had left the room, Longarm turned to Sarah and said, "Now look. They're going to bring you up a bath. Have a good soak. They'll bring you up a good dinner. Perhaps they'll send you up a bottle of good wine or whatever you ask for. Ask for whatever you want. They'll bring you up some clean clothes. I want you to rest."

She looked fearful. She asked, "Where are you going? What are you going to do?"

He said, "I've got to get down to the telegraph office and make some arrangements. I don't know how long it's going to take. I'll be back as quickly as I can. Nothing is going to happen to you."

Surprisingly, she said, "What about that poor horse? The one I was riding?"

That made him smile. He said, "That horse is past the danger. When I bled him, it cooled him off and he didn't founder. I'll see that the horses are well taken care of, so don't worry about it."

She put her hands down along the inside of her thighs and looked up at him ruefully. She said, "I don't think I'm going to be good for anything for a while. I think I'm rubbed raw."

He laughed at her. He said, "Don't worry about that right now. I know you've been under a nervous strain; you've ridden a horse astride for the first time in your life and for a long ways. Sarah, you did real good. You not only saved

119

your life, I think you may have saved mine. Now we have to stop Richard before he can get up to any more devilment."

She looked up at him anxiously. She said, "I know I'm being silly but will you just kiss me before you go?"

Longarm leaned down and gave her a tender, soft kiss on the lips and then he turned. He said, "I have to hurry."

"I understand."

He opened the door. "Lock this door behind me and keep it locked unless you know who it is on the other side."

"Yes."

Then he was out the door and hurrying down the stairs. He walked rapidly through the lobby and out the front door. The boy from the stable was standing there holding the horses' heads. Longarm flipped him a silver dollar. The boy caught it in the air. Longarm said, "Take that dun on into the stable and cool him out and feed him up. I'm going to have to use this roan for about another hour or so and then I'll drop him off at the stable. I want both of them given real special care. You *comprende*?"

"*Si, señor. Yo comprendo.*"

Longarm mounted the roan and turned him toward the other side of town where the railway station and the telegraph station were located. He knew the roan was almost played out so he held down the impulse to put the horse into a gallop and only asked him for a fast walk. It was just as well because he knew he had a hell of a telegram to compose and send Billy Vail. He spent the time that it took him to get to the train depot trying to compose the telegram in his head. It sounded confusing even to him. He had no idea what Billy Vail would make of it.

He tied his horse and went up the steps to the telegraph office and asked for a blank. He walked over to the writing desk. From the looks of things, it might just take more than one blank to get this one off.

The telegram was addressed to Billy Vail, Chief Marshal, Denver, Colorado. It requested immediate delivery at whatever location Mr. Vail was at. The telegram read:

URGENT YOU CONTACT FEDERAL BANKING AUTHORITIES IN SAN ANTONIO STOP URGENTLY REQUEST THEY COMPLY WITH ANY SCHEME PUT FORTH BY JUDGE RICHARD HARDING TO EXCHANGE PRISONER EARL COMBS FOR ME STOP HARDING WILL HAVE LETTER FROM ME INDICATING I AM A PRISONER STOP HE WILL ALSO HAVE MY BADGE STOP I EXPECT HE WILL HAVE SOME PROPOSAL WHEREBY HE CAN FREE ME AND ALSO GET THE INFORMATION FROM COMBS AS TO WHERE HE HAS HIDDEN THE $200,000 THAT HE STOLE FROM THE FEDERAL BANKING SYSTEM STOP I AM NO LONGER A PRISONER BUT HAVE ESCAPED AND AM IN LAREDO STOP IT IS VITAL THAT JUDGE RICHARD HARDING NOT KNOW THIS STOP HARDING IS A CROOK STOP HARDING IS A MURDERER STOP HARDING IS THE ONE THAT TOOK ME HOSTAGE STOP IS NECESSARY HE BE ALLOWED TO PROCEED WITH HIS PLAN STOP YOU MUST PERSUADE THE FEDERAL BANKING AUTHORITIES IN SAN ANTONIO TO RELEASE COMBS TO HIM STOP I AM GOING TO INTERCEPT BOTH OF THEM AT THIS END I HAVE EVERY REASON TO BELIEVE HE WILL MAKE STRAIGHT FOR LAREDO STOP REQUEST THAT YOU ALSO NOTIFY ANY U.S. DEPUTY MARSHAL IN SAN ANTONIO WHO IS CONNECTED WITH THIS MATTER TO FOLLOW HARDING AND ANYONE ELSE WITH HIM AND NOTIFY ME IN LAREDO OF HARDING'S MOVEMENTS AND WHAT TRAIN HE WILL BE TAKING AND WHEN HE CAN BE EXPECTED IN LAREDO STOP URGENT HARDING NOT GET WIND THAT I AM FREE STOP BILLY, YOU BETTER NOT LET ME DOWN ON THIS ONE STOP OR I WILL WRING YOUR SCRAWNY NECK STOP I WANT THAT

121

SON OF A BITCH STOP YOU BETTER NOT MAKE ANY MIS-
TAKES STOP URGENT YOU WIRE ME, IMMEDIATELY TO-
NIGHT, $500 STOP YOU BETTER NOT BE OUT OF TOWN
STOP

The telegram took three blanks. He took the forms over
and handed them to the operator, a vinegary-looking old man
wearing black sleeve guards. The surprised operator read the
forms over, one by one in order. He glanced up at Longarm.

He said, "Who's sending this?"

Longarm said, "It's signed Custis Long, U.S. Deputy
Marshal."

"How am I supposed to know you're a deputy marshal?"

Longarm pulled out the revolver he had taken from Chulo.
He didn't like the feel of it. It was not a .44 caliber, but a
.45. It didn't have the same feel in his hand and it didn't fit
his holster, which had been handcrafted for his own pistol,
a revolver. He reminded himself that Richard Harding had
taken it from him and it was probably at the damned ranch.
But the .45 would have to do. He showed it to the telegraph
operator.

Longarm said, "For the time being, this is my badge. Now
send the damned telegram or do I have to do it myself?"

The skinny operator swallowed visibly, his Adam's apple
going up and down. He said, "Well, you ain't got to get
huffy about it, Marshal."

Longarm said, "I ain't huffy. I'm just in a hurry. It's
nearly eleven-o'clock. That makes it midnight in Denver.
The man I am sending the telegram to is nearly older than
you are and probably goes to bed with the chickens. I'd hate
to have to wake him up too late, the shock might stop his
heart."

The operator said, "You ain't supposed to say 'son of a
bitch' in one of these wires. This here is U.S. government

wire it's being sent over, even though it belongs to the telegraph company."

"That's fine. 'Son of a bitch' is a federal word being sent
by a federal officer over federal wire. Now send it!"

The operator swallowed again. He said, "Yes, sir."

The telegraph came to $12, which Longarm believed was
the most he had ever paid to send a wire. He could, of course,
claim government privilege, but he had given the man such
a fright that he had decided to pay it anyway. It would just
be another thing for Billy Vail to bitch about on his expense
voucher. When the telegraph was gone, Longarm said,
"Now, I'm down at the the River Hotel. Any wires that come
for me, Custis Long, had better reach me. Fast."

The operator looked up at him, surprised. He asked, "Are
you the one they call Longarm?"

Longarm said, "Yes."

The telegraph operator said, "Well, why in the hell didn't
you say so in the first place? I would have been glad to have
this thing sent off ten minutes sooner. Hell, word is that
you're a pretty good man."

"Well, this pretty good man is about whipped. I need
some supper and about half a bottle of whiskey and a bath
and some decent clothes."

As he was about to turn away, the telegraph operator said
curiously, "Is Judge Richard Harding really a crook?"

Longarm whipped around. He said, "You know what will
happen to you if word of that goes outside of this office."

The telegraph operator said, "It ain't going outside this
office, but what you said in this telegram just goes along
with what a lot of folks in this town have been thinking."

Longarm nodded. "I'm glad to hear that. Now where is
there a haberdashery open this time of night where I can get
some clean clothes?"

The telegrapher said, "Well, should be a couple of places

down near the middle of town still open where you can get some jeans and a shirt, if that be all you're wanting. But say, Marshal, something you might want to know. I ain't been on duty all that long but seems like I heard that Judge Harding come in on the afternoon train. I didn't see him myself, you understand?''

Longarm squinted his eyes at the man. He asked, ''You just heard it?''

''It was just kind of passed on, you know, like it was not of any importance. I heard one of the loading-dock employees say something about having seen Judge Harding.''

Longarm bit his lip. He said, ''What the hell is today, anyway?''

The telegrapher said, ''Friday.''

Longarm wheeled around on his heels. ''Thanks.''

He went out the door and down off the platform and mounted the tired horse. If Harding had come in, there was nothing he could do about it. He simply had to wait until he could get confirmation from whatever federal officer Billy Vail could reach in San Antonio. Maybe he would hear tomorrow. It was a big country and he couldn't go dashing here and there looking for a shadow. But he did need to get out of that shadow's clothes. If he was sick of anything, he was sick of wearing Judge Richard Harding's ill-fitting clothes. He went to the store and bought new clothes.

He left the tired horse off at the hotel livery and then walked around the hotel and into the lobby. At the desk, he left word that he wanted a bath sent up to his room and also a steak with all that went with it and a bottle of whiskey. After that, Longarm climbed the stairs to the second floor and went down to his room and let himself in and pitched the parcels he had bought at the general mercantile on the bed. His room and Sarah's shared a connecting door. He unlocked it with a key and opened it slowly, giving a gentle rap as he did. She was up, sitting on the side of her bed in a kind of flannel nightgown. There was a bathtub still in the middle of the room with towels scattered about. She looked wan and drawn but still pretty even with wet hair and no makeup. He came forward, skirting the tub, and leaned down and kissed her lightly.

He said, "You look about tuckered out."

She said, "I am. Did you have any luck?"

"I don't know, honey. All I was doing was getting off a telegram to try and get some information. It will be a little while."

"I thought I was going to go to sleep waiting for you," she said.

"You should have."

"I wanted you to hold me."

He sat down on the bed beside her and put his left arm around her shoulders and held her close. He said, "You were a brave woman, today."

She looked up at him and smiled. "You were the brave one. You were the one that did it all. How did you make that bomb?"

He shrugged, smiling a little. "Mostly by guess and by golly."

"It sure worked," she said. "I see now why you wanted me to try and get under the bed. Gosh, did you see what it did to Miguel?"

Longarm said, "That even surprised me. In fact, I heard a couple of those pieces whiz over my head just as I was falling to the floor. If I had been standing where I'd been, me and them would have connected."

Sarah said timidly, "Honey, I—" She stopped.

He said, "What?"

"I would like to but I don't think I can."

"What?"

125

She blushed slightly. "You know. Make love."

Longarm said, "Oh, I reckon we're both a little too tired for that."

"Yes, but there's this." With hands that trembled slightly, she pulled her gown up past her knees and on up past her cream-colored thighs. She spread her legs slightly. The inside of her thighs were rubbed raw.

Longarm said, "My heavens. That's terrible. We've got to get some liniment on that."

"You see, I don't think I could grip you with my legs."

He smoothed her hair. He said, "Honey, don't you worry about that. I'll go downstairs in just a minute and get some kind of ointment."

She said, "If I could just sleep." Then she suddenly turned her head toward a table at the back of the room. "Oh, by the way, they brought your things from when you were here before."

Longarm turned to look and there sat his valise, the one he had left in the hotel when he had gone to get a drink some days ago. The one he had used to go to Mexico City and come back. The valise contained clean clothes, his derringer, and another revolver, the mate to the one that Harding had taken away from him.

He slapped his forehead with the palm of his hand. "I'll be damned. I just spent sixteen dollars on clothes, closer to seventeen actually, that I didn't have to spend. Damn it. But at least now I know I have a pistol in there that I can make good use of."

He got up and crossed swiftly to the valise and unbuckled it and opened it wide. There on top, where he had left it, was his .38-caliber derringer. He took it out and quickly shoved it inside his concave belt buckle, slipping it under the steel snap that held it in place. After that, he rummaged down through his shirts and jeans and found the mate to his

126

missing revolver. It felt good as he pulled it out of the valise. He immediately took Chulo's pistol out and laid it on the table and returned his own to its rightful place in his holster. Then he thought to take it back out, click open the gate, and spin the cylinder to make sure it was fully loaded. He rummaged around in the bottom of the valise and found the box of .44-caliber cartridges which was still half full. He opened the box and took out six and then six more cartridges. He put six in his right front jeans pocket and six in his right front shirt pocket. It felt good to be equipped again. He rummaged around in his clothes, feeling toward the bottom because that's where the cleaner ones were, and pulled out a blue shirt that he particularly liked and then felt still farther until he found a clean pair of jeans. He laid those on the table and then searched around and got out some clean socks. Just as he was about to draw them out, his knuckles hit something hard, and to his delight, he found a full bottle of the precious Maryland whiskey. Now he remembered that he had been saving it for the happy occasion when he would finally get off the damned train and get loose from that damned Earl Combs. But things had been so rushed and jumbled that he'd forgotten about it and instead had gone to a saloon to buy a bottle of whiskey. There he had met a man who wanted him to go get a horse in Mexico and had ended up back in Laredo with a woman with chafed and chapped thighs. It would make a fine story to tell his grandchildren one day, if they were pretty broad-minded children.

Without pause, he walked over to the table beyond the bed where there was a pitcher and a basin and a couple of glasses. He took one of them, uncorked the whiskey, poured it half full, and then drank the lot of it down in two gulps. He said, looking at Sarah, "Aw, that tastes so good. Do you drink whiskey, Sarah?"

She shook her head quickly. "No, it's too strong."

"Did you get dinner?"

"Oh, yes. They brought me some nice roast chicken and some vegetables and a glass of wine. It was wonderful. They've taken the dishes away and they're supposed to come back for the bathtub."

Longarm said, "I'm going down now to try and get you some salve. When they come for the bathtub, tell them to pull it on into my room."

She said, "If I can stay awake that long."

"I'll be right back," he said.

In the end he had to make do with some Neet's Foot Oil out of the livery stable. It was mostly used to grease saddles and to work into tender spots on horses' knees and their hocks. He figured it would do Sarah some good on her chafed legs.

When he got back up to her room, he found that the bathtub had been pulled into his room and a bucket of steaming water was standing nearby. Also, his supper had been set up on a table and covered with a cloth. He ducked into Sarah's room for a moment. She was already in bed under the covers more than half asleep. He sat down on the edge of the bed and pulled the covers back and carefully lifted her nightgown up. She seemed to barely notice. Her eyes only fluttered slightly, but never opened fully. He pulled her legs apart gently because he knew she was sore, and, as carefully as he could, he began to rub the oil into her bruised and tormented flesh. She had taken a bad pounding from the four-hour ride. But even as cruelly treated as her skin had been, he couldn't help but notice the shapeliness of her legs, the purity of her skin tone, and the light brown thatch where her legs joined. He tried not to notice because the woman had had a rough time, but he caught small glimpses through the sparse thatch of hair of the faint pink and red of the vulva and lips of her vagina. He would not allow himself to become aroused. Instead, he coated her liberally with the oil before he pulled her gown down and pulled the covers back up and then tucked them around her neck. He kissed her softly on the lips and walked quietly out of her room, leaving the door open, and into his own.

He didn't know whether to eat first or to bathe. Either his steak or his bath water would likely get cold. In the end, he took a very quick bath, soaping and rinsing as fast as he could, and then dried off thoroughly and slipped into a clean pair of his own jeans. He kicked Judge Harding's pants and shirts over into a far corner. After that, he sat down at the table and ate the big steak and the potatoes and green beans and canned tomatoes that they had fixed for him.

When he was done with that and felt about half human again, he poured himself a generous amount of the Maryland whiskey, lit a cigarillo, and settled back to relax for the first time in a long while. He didn't feel he could do any real thinking about the judge and his plan. First of all, he didn't have enough information to know what the judge might have been up to or how far along he had come or what he might have accomplished. The telegraph clerk had said he'd heard that Judge Harding had arrived on the afternoon train. Longarm doubted that. A lot of well-meaning people were very anxious to help the law, especially a federal officer, but all too often their help came in the form of misleading information that they wished was true. Through his long years of experience, Longarm had figured out that there were a great number of people out in the world who wanted to be in the know, to feel self-important, to be a part of the action. They seldom were.

He didn't spend much time ruminating about where Harding might be or what he might be up to. He needed good solid information and he needed some action on Billy Vail's part. He didn't think Harding would simply be allowed to depart with the prisoner, Earl Combs, on Harding's say-so alone. As he told him from the very beginning, they didn't swap embezzlers, especially ones that got away with $200,000, for United States deputy marshals that they paid $100 a month.

Longarm finished his drink and his cigarillo and realized how tired he was. It had not been a pleasant five or six days, or whatever time it had been. The days had run together so he wasn't even sure how long it had been, but he had done one thing he hadn't known he could do. He had made one hell of a bomb.

He took a quick look in on Sarah. She was sleeping peacefully under the dim glow of the lamp he had trimmed low for her. He didn't want the room completely dark in case she woke up and was frightened.

He turned his own lamp out and climbed into bed, grateful to be in a room that wasn't so damned white.

They ate breakfast together in Sarah's room. He was not yet willing for her to be seen in public in case she would be recognized and word would somehow get to Harding, wherever he was. It was around nine o'clock. They had both slept late. Longarm had gone downstairs and sent a smart young man over to the federal judge's office to inquire about Harding. He had come back to report that the people who worked in the judge's office had said he was out of town and wasn't expected back for several days.

Sarah was anxious to go out and buy some clothes of her own but she had understood when Longarm had explained why that wouldn't be possible until the right time. Nevertheless, she looked very good in the clothes that Martin Silver had borrowed for her. Longarm had a pretty good idea that they were the property of some whore who worked around the hotel, but he wasn't going to tell Sarah that. She had already commented on how fancy the underwear was that had been provided for her. Longarm had kept a straight face and said yes, that he reckoned that ladies in Laredo were given to that sort of garment.

They were eating eggs and ham and biscuits with a big pot of coffee. Sarah had just finished saying that she could have slept another ten hours as tired as she was.

Longarm said, "That's what excitement and nerves and just plain old out-and-out fear will do for you. Also, I reckon that the horseback ride didn't help too much. How are the insides of your legs?"

She said ruefully, "They are still a mess. Did you put something on me last night? They feel oily."

Longarm laughed at that. He said, "Yes. I didn't think you woke up. Yes, I got some . . . well, actually, it's saddle oil. It was the only thing I could find. I figured it would keep the skin from drying out and cracking and maybe blistering. It was the only thing I could think of."

She reached over and covered his hand. "That was very sweet of you," she said.

He eyed her. The clothes, although they didn't quite fit, certainly set off her figure, especially her bosom. He could envision those big white cantaloupe-sized breasts with their big strawberry tips nestling inside that silk and satin. It made his mouth water in a way that it seldom did at breakfast.

She wanted to know what he was going to do and he had to simply shrug, shake his head, and say he didn't know. He said, "I'm waiting on information before I can act. What has me worried is that he got such a hell of a start on us, but I do believe that his business in San Antonio is going to take some time. I gave him some help last night, sort of greased the rails. Maybe it will work but maybe it won't. The sticky thing is, can it be done without him being tipped off? If the

131

wrong person gets hold of the telegram that I sent to my boss, it will blow the whole thing sky high.''

She asked, puzzled, "I don't understand why you don't just arrest Richard for what he's done to you and for what he did to me. Isn't that enough?''

He nodded. "Yes, that would get him some years in the Cross Bar Hotel, but that ain't the way my job works, Sarah. A U.S. deputy marshal is supposed to throw a big net and make a big catch. I could reel the judge in without much trouble, but the idea is that I'm supposed to get the embezzler, whom we already got, but I'm supposed to catch him in the same net and get him to tell me where the two hundred thousand dollars is and then bring the whole bunch in along with the money.''

"That sounds like a tall order," she said.

"It is, but I've got a boss who's about as tall as a shot glass and damned near as smart. Certainly he is hardheaded and he thinks I ought to be able to do these things in my sleep, so if I come back without cleaning the plate, he ain't going to be pleased and he'll send me off to Montana or somewhere to find somebody who's been stealing sheep in the middle of a blizzard. This is a tricky play, make no mistake, but it's got to be tried.''

She shrugged. "I'm quite sure I'll never understand any of it.''

Longarm was about to speak when he heard a knocking on his door. He got up, went through the connecting door, and answered the summons. It was a boy from the telegraph office. He handed Longarm a telegram and Longarm handed him a quarter. Longarm walked back to the table, tearing the envelope open. Inside was a message that was nowhere near as long as the one he had sent Billy but was a long one for Billy. It said:

YOUR URGENT REQUEST URGENTLY ACTED ON STOP
HAVE YOU GONE INSANE STOP WAS VERY CAREFUL TO
SEND YOUR INFORMATION TO A PARTY I TRUST STOP
WHAT IN HELL ARE YOU UP TO STOP HAVE NOT RE-
CEIVED WORD BACK FROM SAN ANTONIO YET STOP WILL
ADVISE SOON AS STOP HAVE WIRED DEPUTY MARSHAL
IN SAN ANTONIO TO PICK UP MOVEMENTS OF JUDGE
HARDING STOP HE WILL ADVISE YOU BY WIRE STOP WHO
ARE YOU CALLING AN OLD SON OF A BITCH STOP AM
GOING TO BE VERY INTERESTED TO LEARN HOW YOU
MANAGED TO GET YOURSELF TAKEN HOSTAGE STOP YOU
BETTER NOT SHIP ANY HORSES BACK HERE AT GOVERN-
MENT EXPENSE STOP DON'T SEND ME NO MORE TELE-
GRAMS THAT TAKE HALF THE NIGHT TO READ STOP YOU
WOKE ME UP STOP AM COMPLYING WITH YOUR REQUEST
FOR $500 STOP YOU BETTER BE ABLE TO ACCOUNT FOR
EVERY PENNY OF IT STOP YOU BETTER BE DEAD RIGHT
ABOUT THIS FEDERAL JUDGE OR YOU ARE GOING TO BE
DEAD STOP

It was signed Billy Vail, Chief Marshal, Denver, Colorado.
Inside the envelope was a voucher from the Western Union
Telegraph Company that was good at any bank in the coun-
try. The amount was $500.

Longarm passed the telegraph over to Sarah for her to
read. He watched her as a frown slowly built upon her face
as she read on down through the words. When she was finished, she gave him a puzzled look and said, "Your boss is
not a very nice man. Doesn't he realize the danger that
you've been put through? Doesn't he have any sympathy for
your plight?"

Longarm laughed. He couldn't help himself. "Darling,
one of Billy Vail's greatest pleasures in life is seeing just
how much danger he can get me into. He does all of his men

that way. I reckon people mistake his orneriness for orneriness and his crankiness for crankiness, but nobody mistakes his plain old meanness for just plain old meanness.''

She looked at him and smiled slightly. ''You're very fond of him, aren't you?''

''It's kind of hard not to be.''

They passed the morning in Sarah's room. There really wasn't anything Longarm could do until he heard from San Antonio. It was difficult sitting in a hotel room with a beautiful woman who was more than willing to play and to do nothing about it. Longarm wanted to make love to Sarah, but the saddle scalding on her tender skin in the exact worst place made it impossible. He had sent out to an apothecary for some proper salve and had taken great pleasure in applying it. She had protested, saying she could do it herself, but he had insisted, for obvious reasons.

The hours passed and then their lunch was brought up. They had roast beef, mashed potatoes with gravy, and green beans, and apple cobbler for dessert. They were eating well, but nothing else was getting done. After lunch, Longarm stood at the window looking down on the big plaza that lay between the town and the river. He could see people busily going about their business. It made him wish all the more that he had something to do. He finally began quizzing Sarah about where Richard would take Earl Combs if he was successful at getting him into his clutches. Sarah had no idea.

She said, ''He has a big house here in Laredo. It's a beautiful place. I know, I lived there for a little while. I assume his present wife is there. Why don't you believe he will take him to the hacienda in Mexico?''

Longarm shrugged. ''I don't know. I just don't think he'll trust himself with such a valuable commodity so deep into Mexico. I think he will try to get the information out of the man somewhere on this side of the border. He's got authority here. Do you know of any other hideouts that he has?"

She thought for a long time. She said, "Well, he sometimes kept rooms in the Palace Hotel. I don't know what that was for, maybe just for other women." She stopped and snapped her fingers. She said, "Oh, wait. There is one other place. He's got what he calls a hunting lodge, but I don't know where it is. It's somewhere outside of town, ten or fifteen miles away."

"A hunting lodge? Somehow your ex-husband doesn't strike me as someone who would be much of a hunter."

"He's not really. I think it was just someplace he could go with his cronies and drink and play cards or where he could take women."

"You have no idea where it is?"

She shook her head. "None."

A little after one o'clock, Longarm got the roan out of the stable, and following the directions that Sarah had given him, he rode to the eastern outskirts of town to have a look at Richard Harding's town house. It was in the tonier part of town, up on top of a small rise that looked down on the river to the south and the town to the west. There were several big homes out there. Longarm rode onto the place on the pretext of asking directions to look the big house over. He reckoned it contained some ten to twelve rooms. There were several hired hands about the place keeping the yard and the shrubbery up and working in the garden, but he didn't see anything that would resemble a pistolero. As he was about to leave, he saw a young woman on the front porch. She appeared to be in her mid-twenties. Longarm guessed she was the wife that Richard Harding had taken when he had condemned Sarah to a living death. She was pretty enough, Longarm thought, but he wondered what kind of a marriage she had ended up in.

While he was out, Longarm took the opportunity to stop

at a bank and trade the voucher for $500. After that, he rode back to the hotel, put the horse up in the livery stable, and then went to wait with Sarah. They spent the time talking about Richard Harding, with Longarm struggling to gain every ounce of information about the man from a woman who really didn't know him. It was hard going.

Then, at about four o'clock, there came a knock on the door to his room. Longarm answered it. It was another telegram for him. He opened the wire quickly and looked to see who it was from. It was from a Chet Smith, a United States deputy marshal in San Antonio, Texas.

Chapter 10

Without moving from his spot in the doorway, Longarm quickly read the telegram from the U.S. deputy marshal in San Antonio.

FEDERAL JUDGE HARDING IN COMPANY WITH THREE OTHER MEN LEFT SAN ANTONIO THIS DATE AT 4 P.M. ON THE SOUTHBOUND TRAIN STOP TICKET AGENT I QUESTIONED SAID ALL TICKETS FOR THE PARTY WERE FOR LAREDO STOP ONE OF THE MEN WAS EARL COMBS, WHO WAS MANACLED STOP OTHER TWO MEN WERE DESCRIBED BY JUDGE HARDING TO FEDERAL TREASURY OFFICIALS HERE AS FEDERAL COURT BAILIFFS STOP RELEASE OF PRISONER COMBS WAS DONE PER INSTRUCTIONS FROM CHIEF MARSHAL BILLY VAIL STOP HARDING MAKING CLAIM HE CAN FREE CAPTURED DEPUTY MARSHAL AND RECOVER EMBEZZLED MONEY STOP WILL STAND BY FOR ANY FURTHER ORDERS STOP

Longarm read the telegram again and then once more. Then he walked thoughtfully back into Sarah's room and sat down at the table where he had a bottle of whiskey and a glass. He poured himself out a drink and then sat there thinking.

Sarah came up behind him. She said, pointing to the telegram, "Is that some sort of news?"

Longarm nodded slowly. He said, "Yes."

"Is it good news?"

He looked up at her and smiled thinly. "It's going to make things a little tricky. Your ex-husband is due in here tonight. I think the train arrives around eight, that is, if this is where he is coming. There's one stop between here and San Antonio and that's at Hondo. He could get off there and go to Brownsville or Del Rio. The best thing I can do is wait and see what happens. But I don't know how I'm going to follow a man who knows me."

She said, "He'll go home. Why not just go to his house and wait?"

Longarm said, "I don't think this is the kind of business that he wants his new bride to know that he's involved in and I don't think he'll be parading the three men with him around town."

"Who are these three men?"

Longarm shook his head. "One is an embezzler who has two hundred thousand dollars that old Richard would like to get his hands on. I would reckon the other two are a couple of pistoleros. Unfortunately, the man who sent this—" he waved the wire in the air—"didn't say if they were Mexicans or what. I don't know, but he may have a couple of hard boys from this side. I don't know quite what to do. I guess the only thing I can do is to be standing somewhere near that depot when the train gets in tonight and keep an eye out to see what happens."

138

She said, "What if they start back across the border to the hacienda?"

Longarm gave a shudder. He said, "Well, I reckon that I'll just be obliged to go with them." He got up. It was 4:45 by his watch. "The first thing I have to do is go get me a good horse. We nearly rode those two old nags to death. They need a rest."

Longarm knew a horse trader who was about halfway honest, a commodity not that common in Laredo. He left the hotel and walked the four or five blocks to where the man had a small horse lot and stable. For $200, he bought a six-year-old bay gelding that wasn't much to look at but that Longarm knew had a lot of staying power in him and also some quick speed. He borrowed a saddle from the trader, mounted the horse, and put him through his paces, making sure he was nimble enough to get around in heavy brush and also strong enough to force his way if he had to against slow going in the heavy country. The horse had a big-barreled chest and the big hams that showed his quarter-horse blood. He was a horse that would be able to keep up whether Harding was heading for his hacienda twenty miles deep into Mexico or going to his hunting lodge or anywhere else. If Harding went by horse, Longarm felt he had the horse that could stay with him.

When he was satisfied with the animal, he returned the saddle and gave the trader the $200. They made an agreement that if Longarm returned the horse within a week in the same condition he had left in or better, the trader would buy him back for $175. It would be a good deal for the trader. Longarm figured the horse would fetch four or five hundred up country somewhere, maybe even in Denver, but, of course, that would mean another squabble with Billy Vail about him shipping an animal at government expense. Never mind that he'd had to pay for the telegram out of his own pocket and never mind that he'd lost a revolver that would cost $75 to replace.

The trader had thrown in a halter and lead rope, so Longarm walked back to the hotel's livery stable leading the animal. He took the bridle off the roan he had been riding and adjusted it to fit the big bay gelding. Then he took off the saddle blanket and the saddle and adjusted them both to fit the new horse. He left the bay loosely girted in a stall by himself and gave the boy a dollar to make sure that he got well fed and watered and to make sure that he was kept ready to go.

Now there didn't seem to be anything left to do but to wait until eight o'clock that night for the train to come in. After that, all he could do was to follow wherever Judge Harding led. The only fear in his heart was that Harding might have bought a ticket for Laredo but never arrive there, going instead to some unknown location. That would put an end to the whole matter and Longarm could expect to spend the rest of his career searching for the judge and the embezzler and whoever else was with Harding. He didn't even want to think about what Billy Vail would say to him if he let the two culprits slip through his fingers.

Sarah became increasingly nervous as dusk fell and the time stretched toward eight o'clock. The idea of her husband being back in the same town as her frightened her so that she trembled at times. Longarm did his best to reassure her but her only response was to beg him to stay with her and not go out. He answered her that, of course, he had to go because neither she nor anyone else would be safe so long as a crooked federal judge was in office and free. He said, "Sarah, that man has got to be punished. Not only for what he did to you and to me. Do you have any idea how many people, innocent people perhaps, are now serving time or were hung because he's just a mean son of a bitch? Folks

140

like that have got to be stopped. I've got to stop him, Sarah. You're going to have to be brave. You're in no danger. He has no idea you're in this hotel, and Martin Silver will make sure that your room is watched. No one can get through that door. No one. I'll leave you a pistol. You can shoot one. You may not think you can, but you can. I'll cock it for you so all you'll have to do is aim it and pull the trigger."

Slowly Sarah began to calm down. Longarm gave her a weak drink of whiskey and water. After she got that down, she seemed better. They had dinner sent up again and ate well on chicken and rice and some mixed vegetables.

Longarm questioned her again about where Harding's hunting lodge could be. More and more he was convinced that was where the man would head with his prisoner. An out-of-the-way place where he could, at his leisure, convince Earl Combs to tell him where he had hidden the money, and also an out-of-the-way place where Earl Combs could be disposed of once he had given Harding the information he sought. Two hundred thousand dollars was a hell of a lot of money. Longarm thought there was very little Harding wouldn't do to get his hands on that sum.

But Sarah wasn't really sure where the hunting lodge was, rack her brain as she would. She said, "You must remember, Custis, that I wasn't here that long. It wasn't long before I was in exile, before he caught me, before I nearly went crazy with longing and grief and the desire to flee. Now, of course, I can only look back and wonder how I could have been so stupid as to not have run away from the man. But I really don't know exactly where the hunting lodge is located."

To the best of her recollection, it had been west of town some ten or fifteen miles and down by the river. She said, "I somehow have the feeling that it was on an island somewhere near a wide part of the river. Something that Richard said makes me think that, but I can't be sure. He was drunk

141

one night and bragging about what they had done with the women they had there. Apparently they had taken out of the jail a lot of the women that Richard had sentenced and brought them down to the hunting lodge. There was something about making them swim out to the lodge, but I don't know. It's been so long and I really had no reason to pay attention.''

Finally it was time to leave. Longarm made it swift and abrupt. There was nothing else to talk about. He cocked Chulo's pistol, showed her how to pull the trigger, and said, ''Keep this door locked and don't let anybody in. Don't worry about how long I'll be gone because I don't know. Could be that he's not going to come and I'll be right back. But if I'm not, don't think the worst. I'm a hard man to kill.''

She smiled bravely at Longarm and gave him a kiss. She saw him through the door and then locked it behind him.

He left the hotel, got his horse, and rode down to the depot. He tied the horse on the freight end of the depot platform, well back in the shadows. It was a moonlit night, too moonlit for Longarm's purposes. The moonlight had helped them the night before in their escape, but now it was a hindrance to his plans. He stepped up on the passenger platform and looked down the tracks. It was ten minutes before eight and there was still no sign of the train. He walked about looking for a place where he could hide and watch the passengers as they disembarked from the train. But the passenger platform was too well lit. He could be easily spotted. Then, a sudden thought occurred to him. He looked inside the glass and saw that the same telegrapher was on duty that had been there when he sent the telegram to Billy Vail. He went inside the passenger part of the depot and then ducked quickly into the office where the telegrapher sat.

The man looked up as Longarm entered and said, ''Well,

you may be the famous Longarm, but you ain't supposed to be in here."

Longarm figured he could trust the man—hell, he *had* to trust him. He said, "Look, I have every reason to believe that Judge Richard Harding is coming in on the eight o'clock train. I don't want him to see me. I'm going to get down here on the floor next to your desk where I can't be seen. Can you see where they unload the passengers?"

The telegrapher leaned over and spit tobacco juice into a spittoon. He said, "Yeah, I can see 'em. I can tell you right quick if he gets off."

"Good," Longarm said. "You're going to be my eyes."

The telegrapher leaned back and looked at Longarm. He said, "What's the job pay?"

Longarm said, "It's good for one free pass to get out of jail, in case I ever put you in."

The telegrapher nodded. "Sounds damned good." He nodded his head toward the corner. "If you'll sit down there on the floor where that wastebasket is, ain't nobody gonna be able to see you, even if they come in from out there on the platform. I can watch and I'll tell you what they do."

Longarm said, "I'm obliged." He moved the wastebasket and sat down in the corner. The glass front of the telegrapher's booth did not run all the way across. Where he was sitting, the wall was solid on the platform side and solid halfway across on the passenger waiting-room side.

Longarm took off his hat and settled down. He said, "See any sign of the train?"

The telegrapher looked down the track. He said, "I can barely make out a light flashing. That'll be it, and right on time, too."

It was not a long wait. After a few minutes, Longarm felt the floor begin to tremble beneath him. A moment or two later it seemed, the train came smoking and clanging and huffing and puffing and thundering and squealing into the station. He heard it sigh to a stop as it expelled steam from its boiler.

The telegrapher said, "The passengers are starting to get out of two cars, one right beside you and one down the track. A lady got off . . . that ain't him. Another lady got off . . . that ain't him. Well, there's a man got off one car down the track. He's done got off and looking back up. Another man's got off. Here comes a man down . . . got chains on his wrists or handcuffs or whatever you call them."

Longarm tried to keep the excitement out of his voice. "That would be them."

"Yep. And there's good old Judge Richard Harding, the last one out. He's carrying a valise. The others, well, two of them have saddlebags and the one with the manacles, he ain't carrying nothing."

Longarm asked, "Well, what are they doing now?"

The telegrapher watched for a moment. "They're a-talkin'." He paused for a moment. "Now they're looking around. One of them that ain't the judge and ain't the one in the handcuffs is walking down this way and having a look. He's done gone by. I can't see him no more. The other one that ain't the judge and ain't the one in handcuffs is looking off the other end of the passenger platform. Now he's coming back. Now here comes the other one back. Now they're all talking and they're all walking toward the edge of the platform toward the steps on the town side."

"Have they stepped down yet?" asked Longarm.

"No. Well, one of them has. He's going down the steps and now he's starting down the road," said the telegrapher. "The other three are just standing there. Now he's out of my sight and they're watching him."

"What about Harding? Was it Harding?"

"Nope. It was one of them that . . . well, let's just call him

144

one of them that has a gun on. The other one with the gun and the one with the handcuffs is there and Judge Harding is there and they are just standing there, waiting.''

''Where do you suppose that other one is going?''

The old man said, ''Well, I don't know about you, Marshal, but if I had just come in on the train and no one had met me, I'd be going to the livery stables to get a buggy or a buckboard or some horses.''

Longarm chuckled slightly. ''We could use a man like you. I like the way you think.''

The telegrapher said dryly, ''You didn't like it so well the other night when you were showing me that big pistol for a badge.''

''Someday I will tell you what kind of mood and shape I was in. Maybe then you'll understand.''

''Oh, it didn't bother me none. I got to tell everybody that I'd had a gun drawn on me by the famous Longarm and made him put it away.''

Longarm chuckled again. ''That you did. Keep watching.''

It was a long wait in terms of anticipation. In minutes, it was only about ten. The telegrapher said, ''Yep. That was it. The one that walked off is pulling up with a buckboard. He's driving a two-horse team. Now the other three are going down the steps. The judge is getting in the front seat with the driver and the other two are getting in the back. The other gunman is shoving the one that's manacled up into the back. By the way, I didn't tell you that the one that has the manacles on has something tied across his mouth. Looks like a handkerchief. It appears they gagged the man.''

Longarm said grimly, ''I don't blame them.''

''They're treating him pretty rough, but they're allowing him to sit up now. He made a motion right then to try and get over the side of the buckboard, but that wasn't very smart because that gunman drug him back right smart.''

"What are they doing now?"

"The driver is starting the horses. Now he's wheeling them around. They are going to head south. In about thirty seconds they're going to be out of my view."

Longarm got to his feet. "I am much obliged to you, sir. I'll see you when I get back. Maybe we'll have a drink and talk about it."

The telegrapher said, "If you're going to follow them folks, you had better get high behind because they are a-movin'. They've already gone out of my sight."

Longarm rushed out of the office and hurried around the building on the track side back toward the freight platform. When he got to the end, he peered around just in time to see the wagon heading south on the town's main street. A building blocked his view so he had to cross the platform to the street side to where he could see. He saw the wagon continue on south and his heart sank. They were headed for the bridge just as sure as shooting. They were going to the hacienda. Damn, he thought. Harding would get there, see the dead bodies, know that Longarm had escaped, and he would be hell to catch after that. It would flush him, sure enough.

Longarm hurried down the steps, caught up his horse, and walked out into the street. He could just barely make out the buggy; it was some five or six blocks ahead of him. He mounted as quick as he could and struck a fast walk, hoping to keep up with the buggy but not get too close. It was continuing on south toward the bridge. He followed for two, three, and then four blocks, watching the buggy. It had already passed through the central part of town and was only a quarter mile from the bridge. He was certain that it would be going across.

But then, to his amazement, the buggy suddenly turned to the right, toward the west. He wasn't sure what that meant. He could only hope that Harding and his party were headed for some country road that ran down along the river in the direction where Sarah had said the hunting lodge might be found.

Even though it was well past eight o'clock, the streets were still crowded and many stores were open. Fortunately, most of the people were up on the sidewalk and he was able to kick his horse into a lope, only now and then having to dodge a wagon or someone who had suddenly decided to dart across his path. He got to the corner where the buggy had turned and slowed his horse to a walk as he cautiously went around. It was dark for the space of a couple of blocks from the overhang of buildings. Then, he got a glimpse of the buckboard moving along at a good clip, having cleared the outskirts of town. He urged his pony forward to keep within good sight of them.

Once away from the town, the country was rolling plains covered with mesquite and cedar thickets and now and again a post oak tree. The bare spaces were taken up by grease-wood bushes and cactus brambles. Longarm could clearly see the white caliche road sneaking its way through the darker heavy overgrowth. The buckboard was about a half mile ahead. He came into the moonlight cautiously, aiming to make sure they didn't see him following behind them. For a short while, he tried to follow off the road, picking his way through the dense growth of stunted trees and plentiful bushes and briars. The going was too slow, and besides, it was scratching his horse across the legs and the chest plate. If he kept it up, the animal would get shy and go to bucking or pitching. He swung back into the road but took his time, going slow, catching occasional glimpses of the buggy ahead as the road wound to the left and now back to the right. If Sarah was right that it was a ten- or fifteen-mile trip then he had plenty of time to follow them. The only thing he worried about was the road forking.

He followed slowly for about an hour, catching glimpses of the buggy only now and then as it continued its westward progress. He calculated they had come at least seven or eight miles from town. The buggy was still moving at a smart trot. Longarm let his horse out a little into a fast walk. He didn't want them to get too far ahead nor did he want them to arrive at the hunting lodge too far in advance of him. Could be they'd get their business done quickly and he'd meet them coming back. He was very anxious to hear what went on in the hunting cabin.

Another hour passed and he thought they should be close, very close. The moon was higher now and casting a good glow. It would be very difficult to get near them without being seen, so he forced himself to maintain a pace a little slower than theirs. A little more than two hours after he had begun to follow them across the countryside, he got one last glimpse and then they seemed to disappear. He rode on ahead, picking up the pace. He had grown used to the movement ahead, the sudden flashes of the buggy as it stood in contrast to the brush it was going through along the road. Now, there was nothing ahead. No movement. In a kind of panic, Longarm urged his horse into a slow lope, conscious of the sound the horse's hooves were making. He could not let them get too big of a lead on him. Just as he was beginning to worry that he might have lost them, he saw a trail lead off to his left toward the river. In the moonlight, he could see the wagon tracks. They looked very fresh in the loose dirt. He pulled his horse up and leaned out of the saddle to study them and then looked toward the river. By squinting his eyes, he could make a small structure separate itself from the treeline. The trees appeared higher down near the river, which, of course, would be the nature of things. He looked back to his right where the road continued. There were no signs of fresh wagon tracks. He had to believe, based on time and distance, that Harding and his cohorts had reached the turnoff to his hunting lodge.

Longarm turned his animal left, holding him to a slow walk. He went perhaps half a mile. Now the outline of the small building was becoming distinct in the night. He guessed it to be no more than a quarter of a mile away, but night distances could sometimes be misleading. He rode on for a couple of hundred yards more and then stopped his horse. He dismounted and led the animal back into the bushes, tying him to a post oak tree that reared up amongst a grove of mesquite. The horse wouldn't have anything to eat or drink, but Longarm didn't expect to be long.

He began to work his way through the bushes toward the cabin. After about ten minutes, he reached the river's edge and he saw why Sarah thought the cabin was on an island. It was actually on a spit of land that ran out into the river like a peninsula. Once toward the center of the river, the patch of land widened out until it was about an acre in size. Set in the middle of that was a one-story lumber and adobe cabin. Its roof was almost flat as were so many in that part of the country. It appeared to be shingled with tar paper. A stovepipe stuck up from the back corner, but there was no chimney for a fireplace. Laredo was not a town where people used fireplaces for warmth, since it seldom got below seventy at any time of the year.

He could see the peninsula that ran out to the big parcel was lower, and he could imagine when the river was up, it would be under water, making the cabin virtually an island. As if to confirm this, a rowboat was tied up at the bank and he could quite easily see the tracks of the buckboard where the wheels had sunk into the soft ground as they had driven the hundred yards to the cabin.

He spent a few moments studying the situation. The door was shut and there were two windows at the front but

149

they were small and high up. It would be difficult for anyone to see him out of those windows. Nevertheless, he didn't want to take the chance of being seen by heading directly for the house. He took his boots off, and holding them in one hand and carrying his revolver in the other, he stepped down into the river water, first up to his knees and then up to his hips. Bending low, he worked his way slowly to the higher ground that the cabin was sitting on. He came up out of the water on the side of the cabin. There was one window that was set like a normal window with a sash, but there was a curtain over it that made it difficult to see inside. He snuck past that and got around to the back of the cabin. There was nothing there except a blank wall.

Behind the cabin was a corral where the two buggy horses had been turned in. There was a small toolshed or feedshed, he didn't know which. The buckboard was sitting close to the back of the cabin. He thought if he could move the buckboard over some five or ten feet, he could use it to get up on the roof, which appeared to be only about ten feet high.

Straining and being as quiet as he could, he picked up the rear of the buckboard and shifted it over until it was almost against the corner of the cabin.

Longarm got up in the buckboard and stood up on one of its sides, but he couldn't quite reach the edge of the roof. He had put his boots back on. He looked around. He walked over and carefully opened the door of the little shed. Inside, he found a busted ladder-back chair. He took it, positioned it in the buggy against the wall of the cabin, and then carefully climbed up its flimsy structure. He was able to get his arms and his shoulders onto the roof, and working slowly, inch by inch, he managed to drag himself up onto the building's top. Once there, he lay flat, his ear pressed to the tar-paper shingles. He could hear a low murmur of voices and now and then a yelp, but he couldn't make out anything distinctly. A thought occurred to him and he went over to the stovepipe that stuck out of the roof. He touched it first and then put his ear to it and found he could distinctly hear what was being said inside.

The first words he heard clearly were in the carefully modulated voice of Judge Richard Harding. He said in a pleasant voice, "Now, Earl. We've been rather easy on you so far. Now, if you don't tell us where the money is, I'm afraid I'm going to have to let these two gentlemen have their way."

Longarm heard the voice of Earl Combs say, "I don't know where the money is, don't you understand? I had a partner. He took the money."

Harding said, "You're lying, Earl"—there was a sound of a sigh—"and I'm getting very tired of it. Jack, you and Morris go ahead."

Longarm heard the faint sounds of a brief struggle. He heard one of the men swearing. A voice said, "Damn it, Morris. Hold his damn hand still. I can't bend that finger back the way I want to with him thrashing about."

Another voice said, "Why in the hell don't we just hit him on top of the head and slow him down some."

Richard Harding's dry voice said, "Yes, Morris. That would be intelligent. Knock him out so he can't feel the pain. I'm sure that he'd tell us then."

There was silence for a moment and then a sudden scream rose and rose until it went into a shriek. Longarm clenched his teeth. He hated what was going on in the cabin, but he knew that they would get the information about where the money was faster than he could. He would wait as long as he could stand it.

There was a sound of someone sobbing and saying, "Oh, my God! Oh, my God!"

Harding's voice said, "Do you see what I mean, Earl?

You're just hurting yourself for no good reason. You are going to tell us where the money is. Go ahead, Jack.''

There came a dim mumble of words, a loud oath, a loud exclamation, and then another scream.

A voice said, "I swear! I don't know where the money is. I swear it." Longarm could hear a sob in the voice. He could actually hear the man sound as if he was crying.

Richard Harding said, "Let's make it a little tougher. Let's start breaking them in two places."

Now the screams came swiftly and violently. They went on for something like two or three minutes. The sounds almost made Longarm sick to his stomach. One thing they did, which was something he didn't think possible, was to make him despise Richard Harding even more.

Finally a voice said, "Judge, this son of a bitch is a harder nut to crack than I thought. Let's say we fire that kitchen stove up and see how he likes petting red-hot cast iron."

Harding said, "That sounds like a good idea, Jack. Go ahead.''

Overhead, Longarm heard the news with some alarm. He didn't know if he'd be able to hear or not. He was not listening at the open end of the stack but at the side. He didn't know what soot and smoke coming up the pipe would do.

A voice said, "Judge, I think this son of a bitch has passed out. He's just laying there."

Longarm heard a thud as if someone had been kicked. "Naw, he was just playing possum. A little nudge in the ribs got his attention."

Harding said, "Get his shoes off and his socks."

The voice that Longarm had learned to recognize as Jack's said, "There, I've got that kitchen stove fired up plenty good. It shouldn't be but a few minutes."

Harding said, "Jack, while we're waiting, it might not be a bad idea to try some splinters under his toenails. I'm a

152

great believer in fire as a pain giver. Look around the cabin here and see if you can find some splinters. Just running one underneath his big toenails might get us some response.''

On the roof, Longarm heard laughter. He doubted any of it was coming from Earl Combs. It was strange to hear this and to feel sorry for the man whom he had been so sick of only a week back. There were no sounds from the cabin for a few minutes and then Longarm heard Jack say, ''Here, Judge. What about this? I've made some shavings off this pine board. Don't you reckon they'd slip up under there and do a pretty good job?''

Harding said, ''Yeah, that's good thinking, Jack. Give it a try.''

Longarm heard some scuffling and struggling and then a scream, though it was more a scream of fear than anguish or pain. Then there was a silence that lasted about thirty seconds. It ended with a cry of such desperation that Longarm didn't know how much longer he could stand it. By now, smoke was pouring out of the chimney along with blinking sparks and pieces of wood ash. He supposed the top of the cast iron stove was already beginning to heat up. He dreaded to think of what they were going to do.

The screaming finally subsided into a whimper and then the whimper into quiet sobs and moans.

Harding said, ''Well, Earl. It's up to you. It's not going to get better. I know you hid that money somewhere.''

Between sobs, Combs said, ''Richard, I ain't got it. I don't know where it is, you've got to believe me.''

The familiar way that Combs addressed Judge Richard Harding made Longarm wonder if perhaps the judge himself had not been involved somehow in the transaction. Perhaps it had been his idea. Perhaps he had lent his authority in some way to the embezzlement. It didn't matter. Longarm's job was to bring them all in and recover the money. That was one of the things he liked about being a deputy marshal, his duty was clear-cut. It wasn't always easy, but at least it was clear-cut.

There were more screams and more sobbing and moaning.

Longarm was listening carefully. He surprised himself by being able to judge that Earl Combs, even though he was being hurt, was not being tortured to the extent that would cause him to reveal where he had hidden the $200,000. They had not yet reached that point of pain that was worth $200,000 to make it stop. He thought, however, the stove just might be the answer.

Richard Harding said, "Well, this is not working. Jack, go test that stove. Spit on it and see how hot it's getting, then get his pants off."

Someone cackled, "Judge, you don't mean you're going to set him on that stove, do you?"

Richard Harding said, "Well, it's a little experiment. Benjamin Franklin said that time was relative. Five minutes with a beautiful woman was different from five minutes sitting on top of a hot stove. I think I'll test that theory out."

Longarm could hear Earl Combs instantly begin to protest, sobbing and begging and whining and moaning. The judge said, "Earl, you can stop it anytime you want to. Just tell us where the gold is or lead us to it."

"You'd just kill me."

Harding laughed. He said, "Why would I want to do that? All I want is the money. You're nothing to me. I have no reason to kill you or keep you alive."

Longarm smiled thinly to himself. The judge was very good at making it sound plausible that he wasn't going to kill you. He knew. The judge had said the same thing to him.

Longarm glanced at the smoke that was coming out of the stovepipe. He could see little flames in it. He reckoned that Jack had filled the firebox full and that it was going like sixty. He didn't doubt that it would begin to glow before very long, and it made him shudder inside to think that they were going to put a man's bare skin onto such a surface.

Harding said, "We're just about there, Earl, and there you are with your bare ass hanging out, about to have it applied to the stove. I'll tell you what. We'll put your hand on it first, and then if you feel like telling us, we won't roast the ass off you. How's that?"

Combs began to scream and yell and curse and moan and cry. Longarm could hear the two men swearing at him. He could hear scuffling. They were apparently trying to take him over to the stove. Jack said, "Damn it, you son of a bitch. Quit fighting it. Quit fighting or I'll break your nose with the barrel of my revolver. Come on, get his arm up behind his back, Morris. Hurry up."

Harding said, "One of you hold him and the other take hold of his left hand by the wrist with both hands. He's going to struggle."

Longarm could hear a sudden sizzle. At first he thought it was the sound of Earl Combs's hand frying but then he heard Jack say, "There, Judge, I poured some whiskey on it. Listen to it sizzle." Almost instantly, Longarm got a strong whiff of vaporized liquor. He wondered what it would to do to Combs's hand.

Harding said, "Touch one finger to it first, boys."

"Judge, it ain't gonna be easy," Jack said. "He's hard to hold. I can't guarantee just one finger."

"Get his hand on it then."

There was a pause and then there was a scream that seemed to almost pierce right through the ceiling and rise high into the sky. In that second, Longarm knew that Earl Combs had reached his point of pain. He began screaming, "I'll tell ya! I'll tell ya! Don't! Stop, please! Oh, my God, I can't stand it! I can't stand it! Help me!"

Richard Harding said, "Where's the money, Earl?"

"The pain! I can't stand it!"

Harding said coldly, "You get a drink of whiskey and you get to ram your hand into a bucket of water the minute you say where the money is. It's up to you."

"It's in the Laredo National Bank." Combs was screaming and crying. He said, between sobs, "It's in a safety-deposit box."

"What's the number of the safety-deposit box?"

"Five-zero-nine."

"All right, boys. Give him a rest. Stick his hands in that bucket of water and give him a shot of whiskey."

Longarm shook his head slowly. The money had been within reach the whole time. Safety-deposit box number 509. That was all he needed to know. Now he could take them in.

He looked around for some way to get them out in the open. The obvious course was to stop up the smoke stack. He took off his hat, looked at it, and then looked at the smoke stack, which was throwing forth dark smoke filled with sparks. It was a forty-dollar hat. He sighed and then thought of something else. Hell, his shirt was only a five-dollar shirt. Better a five-dollar shirt than a forty-dollar hat. As he was taking the shirt off, he could hear Combs still moaning and then he heard Richard Harding say, "Now where is the key to that safety-deposit box, Earl?"

There was a moan and then Combs said, "I don't know. I don't know. I can't think, I'm hurting so bad."

Harding said, "I'm going to ask you one more time, Earl, before your hand goes back on the stove. Where is the key?"

"Let me think. Let me think, please."

Longarm had his shirt stripped off. He wadded it into a ball and then stuffed it down into the stovepipe. Within seconds, the cabin was going to fill up with smoke. He didn't particularly care where the key was—he didn't need the key. He could go in with a court order and get box 509 open. He began to creep toward the front of the cabin. If matters went right, he was soon going to have company.

The front door, he had made certain, was the only exit out of the cabin. Smoke would come boiling out of the stove and they were going to have to come outside. He was going to be sitting right above them when they did. As he crept along the length of the roof, he could hear a commotion beginning inside. He heard someone yell, "Where the hell is all that smoke coming from?" Then he heard muffled curses and swear words.

Somebody yelled, "It's that damned stove! What's the matter with that stove? Somebody open a window!"

He got to the edge and could look down on the ground right in front of the cabin. He put his ear down and heard somebody say, "We're going to smother in here. Christ, somebody open that damn door!"

It was only a few seconds more and the door was suddenly flung open wide and three men came stumbling, one by one, out into the night, coughing and gasping for air. The first two were obviously the men that Judge Harding had referred to as federal court bailiffs. To Longarm's eye, they were common gunmen. Harding was the last one out. They were all three bent over coughing. Longarm could not see a gun on Harding. He was wearing a waistcoat and he might have had a shoulder holster but Longarm didn't think of Harding as the pistol type. He wondered what was happening to Earl Combs. Apparently, they had left him lying on the floor to suffocate. Longarm glanced back at the chimney. He could see his shirt was on fire and in another second it would burn away and the smoke would go up the flue again. He carefully drew his pistol and cocked it. He leaned down over the edge of the roof.

157

He said loudly, "You're under arrest. Raise your hands."

There was a shocked silence as all three men suddenly straightened up and looked around.

Longarm said, "You're under arrest. Hands up."

The gunman farthest from the door glanced up. Instinctively, his hand went to his revolver and he started to draw. Longarm shot him square in the upper chest, the bullet appearing to drive him downward before it knocked him flat over on his back.

The second gunman was just a half second behind his companion. Longarm let the man's gun clear the leather of his holster and start upward before he shot the man. The bullet seemed to catch him just below the neck. He staggered and then fell backward. Longarm was already moving. Richard Harding was staring up. As he fumbled inside his coat, Longarm already had an idea what he was looking for. Without pause, he jumped. He didn't want to kill Harding, he had other plans for him. He watched the man's face come straight up at him as he plummeted downward. He landed a boot on each side of Harding's shoulders. He felt something crunch under his right boot heel and then Harding was going down, crumpling beneath him. Longarm had a very soft landing. He rolled off the man and got quickly to his feet. Harding was lying on the ground, stunned. He looked up, his eyes suddenly fluttering open. Longarm could tell Harding wasn't seeing straight just yet. Then he could see the man's eyes clear as he stared into Longarm's face. For a second, Harding just blinked his eyes, his mouth going slack.

He said, "Why, you . . . you . . ."

Longarm finished it for him. "You son of a bitch. I'm here, Harding. I guess you didn't expect that. Now you and I are going to have some real fun, Mister Brown."

Chapter 11

Longarm's shirt had burned away and the smoke had disappeared up the flue. Now he sat in a chair and Earl Combs was slumped on the floor near the door where he had been when Longarm had prodded Richard Harding back into the room. Harding was sitting on the floor, holding his left shoulder, moaning that his collarbone was broken. Longarm said, "Where's my badge, Harding?"

Harding said, "I don't know."

"I'm going to ask you one more time. I think you've used those very words yourself, haven't you, on Mr. Earl Combs here? I'm going to ask you one more time where my badge is."

Harding looked at him. The man was still unrepentant. He still thought he was on top. He did not know what had transpired to bring about his downfall. He said, spitting out the words, "You've got nothing on me, nothing you can prove. As a matter of fact, I may have you up on charges; you've broken my collarbone. I don't know anything about your badge."

Longarm suddenly reached out and grasped Harding by the left wrist. He began to rotate the man's arm so that he could see the two ends of the broken collarbone turn under the skin. Harding let out a loud scream and writhed on the floor. He couldn't jerk his arm away because it only brought on more pain.

Longarm kept turning the arm as if it was a crank. He said, "Whenever you're ready, I'll stop."

Harding screamed, "It's in my valise! Please, stop!"

Longarm let the arm drop. There was a pigskin leather case against one wall. He said, "Is this it?" Harding nodded dumbly. Longarm took two steps to the case and then set it up on the table. He opened it. It was full of clothes and papers. Toward the bottom, he found his badge. It was still intact. He was about to put it in his shirt pocket when he realized he wasn't wearing a shirt. Instead, he stuffed it in his right pants pocket along with the cartridges that he had taken out of his shirt pocket. He didn't much want to go into town bare-chested so he found a white silk shirt of Harding's and put it on.

"Damn, Richard. It seems as if I'm always borrowing your clothes. I had to wear an outfit of yours out at your ranch just before I killed most of your men."

Harding gave him a hard look. "Go to hell, Longarm."

"No, I believe you're the one who's got the seat reserved for that trip."

Harding said, "You can't do a damned thing to me."

Longarm finished buttoning the shirt and smiled. He said, "You get yourself a good place on the front pew and watch me."

"You don't have a single witness that I had anything to do with you."

Longarm smiled at him. He was not about to mention Sarah to the man. He had a little surprise cooked up for Harding where Sarah was concerned. He said, "Give me that key to those manacles you've got on Combs."

Harding looked at him and said, "Make me."

Longarm reached for the man's left arm and the judge suddenly discovered the key in his waistcoat pocket. Longarm helped Combs to his feet. The man was still moaning and looked half dazed. Longarm unlocked one of the wrist irons and clamped it onto Harding's left wrist.

He said to Combs, "The judge has a collarbone broke on that side. If you jerk on him, it'll hurt him worse than ice water on an aching tooth."

He forced the two out of the cabin ahead of him. They walked through the front door awkwardly, neither one willing to give way to the other. Finally, Longarm shoved Harding on ahead, then he shoved them both past the two dead men and around the corner of the cabin. He made them wait at the edge of the river by the corner of the corral while he put the harness on the two buckboard horses. After that, he led the two horses out and hitched them to the wagon tongue. He climbed up on the seat and bade Harding and Combs get in the back. They did so with many a groan and a cry and a moan. Longarm was enjoying it, especially Harding's plight. He actually almost felt sorry for Combs; not quite, but almost. He did enjoy seeing Harding in pain. Occasionally, Combs would lose his balance as they struggled to get themselves arranged in the buckboard and would jerk on Harding's left arm, which would cause the judge to scream in pain. Before they were quite settled, Longarm slapped the team with the reins and took off in such a way that the two men tumbled over on their sides. That brought more screams. They had broken three of Combs's fingers and had made a bloody mess out of several of his toes. Longarm had thrown the man's boots into the back of the buckboard, but he figured it would be a while before the man was going to be able to walk very far. He had left everything else in the cabin as it was. The judge had wanted his valise but Longarm had denied him the baggage.

They went along up the path to where Longarm had left his horse tied. He got down, fetched the horse and tied him to the back of the wagon, and then got back in and started for town. It was late. He guessed it to be going on midnight, at least, and it would be another two hours before they were back in town.

As they rumbled along under the almost full moon, Longarm turned his head around and said to Earl Combs, "Earl, you can tell me where that key is or not. I can get that box open with a court order, but I can also make things harder on you than they have to be. You're not going anywhere for a long time, and I already know where the money is, so if you want me to make things easier on you, then tell me where the key is."

Combs looked down to the floor of the buckboards. "It's in my heel."

"What?" Longarm said.

"It's in the heel of my right boot. It's in a little hole. All you have to do is pry it off."

Longarm nodded. "That's pretty damned smart, though I don't see why you took that punishment."

Combs said, "I didn't want this son of a bitch to have it."

"Yes, but if I hadn't have come along, he might have gotten a court order to have the box opened himself."

Harding said, "You're damned right. I'm a federal circuit judge, and listen, you little pissant deputy marshal, you better remember that. When this mess gets straightened out, you are in big trouble."

Longarm laughed. "How do you plan to get away with that?"

"I made a deal to fetch you back safely and to get the money from Combs. That's what I've done."

Longarm looked around at him, amused. He said, "Didn't you find it a little funny how they suddenly gave in to your proposal?"

Harding stared back at him, puzzled. He said, "What are you talking about?"

"I reckon you'll find out."

It was almost three o'clock before they finally rolled into Laredo. Longarm had taken it easy on the livery stable buckboard horses. They'd had a forty-mile round trip and he took it as lightly on them as he could. He pulled the buggy up in front of the sheriff's office and then pulled Combs and Harding out of the back and onto the street. He unlocked the cuff on Combs's wrist and quickly jerked both of Harding's arms behind him and handcuffed the loose cuff to his other wrist. Then he shoved both of them toward the sheriff's office. Two deputies were on night duty when he came through the door with his prisoners. He shoved Earl Combs forward.

He said to the young sheriff's deputy standing behind a desk, "I'm Custis Long, U.S. Deputy Marshal." He got out his badge and showed it to the deputy. "And this is Earl Combs. He's a federal prisoner. I want him held until he's picked up by federal authorities. Do you understand?"

The young deputy looked nervous and surprised. He said, "Yes, sir, Marshal Long. I'll lock him up."

Longarm said, "Don't lose him."

"No, sir, I won't." The deputy was staring at Richard Harding. He asked, "Is that Judge Harding you got there?"

Longarm said, "Yes, but I'm not going to put him up in your hotel tonight."

Harding suddenly said, "Deputy, I'm a federal court

163

judge. I demand you arrest this marshal. He is illegally detaining me.''

Longarm took Harding by the left arm so that it would pull on his collarbone and jerked him to the front door. Harding let out a scream. Longarm looked back at the deputy. He said, ''He was a federal circuit court judge but he's not one anymore. He's just a common criminal. I'll be bringing him back in a little while. Until then, watch good over that other one.''

Harding was nervous once they got back into the buckboard. He said to Longarm, ''Listen, what are you going to do with me? If I'm your prisoner, by rights you should have left me in that jail. What are you planning? To take me out in the country and murder me someplace where there're no witnesses?''

Longarm said, ''I've got a better idea than that.''

He pulled the buckboard into the hotel's livery and tossed the reins to the night man. He explained that the outfit belonged to the town livery down the street and wondered if he could get someone to return it. He gave the night man a dollar.

After that, Longarm walked Harding up the steps of the hotel, but at the door, Harding balked. ''I'm not going into the hotel like this. Handcuffed and disgraced? No!''

Longarm opened the door and shoved him forward, so hard that Harding fell to his knees ten feet into the lobby. It was deserted except for the night desk clerk. He looked at Harding and then at Longarm with surprise. He said, ''Marshal, is everything all right?''

''Yeah, it's finally getting all right, but it took its own good time about it.'' Longarm took a few steps toward the desk. ''As well as I recollect, you have always kept a cane or two around here for some of your older guests in case they mislaid theirs, is that right?''

The desk clerk was still looking at Richard Harding. He said, "Yes, sir. We have several. Did you need one?"

Longarm walked over. "Yeah, do you have a good india rubber style there?"

The young man said, "Yes, sir, I do." He handed Longarm a thin handsome cane that was just about the size and the heft and the stiffness that he desired. As he was about to turn away, the desk clerk whispered to Longarm, "Isn't that Judge Harding over there?"

Longarm said in a loud voice, "That's *ex*-judge Harding. Right now, he's a federal prisoner." He walked over to the man and tapped him lightly with the cane. He said, "Get up to your feet, Harding, or I'll jerk you up by your hair."

With his hands handcuffed behind his back, the judge had a hard time struggling up. Finally, Longarm grabbed him by the left arm and pulled him to his feet. The judge gave a small scream of agony. He swore.

Longarm slapped him across the back with the cane, hard enough to feel. "What's the matter with you, Judge? Ain't you got no better manners than to cuss in the lobby of a public place? Now, get on over there to those stairs." He gave the judge another shove, not quite so hard this time.

They went up the stairs, the judge stumbling and complaining about his hands being handcuffed. Longarm said, "You know, that reminds me of my own particular situation about a week ago. Some son of a bitch did me the same way you're rigged up and then set me on a horse and rode me about four or five hours. I'll tell you, my shoulders were sore for days afterward. Is that what you're talking about?"

Harding didn't say anything.

They went down the hall to Longarm's room. He stopped Harding with his arm. As he got his key out, he said to his prisoner, "Now, Harding, we're going in here, into my room. You make any noise or any sound to wake anybody up, I'm going to split your skull for you. Do you understand me?"

Harding turned and looked at Longarm coldly. "You're a bully."

It was all Longarm could do to keep from speaking of Sarah. He said, "Bully, huh? Well, you ought to know about that." He unlocked the door and pushed Harding into the room. As they passed the open door that connected his room to Sarah's, he could see that her room was half lit. He listened quietly for half a moment, making sure she was asleep. He wasn't ready for her just yet and the light from her room gave him enough visibility so that he didn't have to bother with the lamp in his own room.

He got out the key so that he could unlock the cuff from one of Harding's wrist. As the man's arm swung forward, Longarm said, "You better not get any big ideas, Harding, or I'll break that other collarbone of yours."

He took off Harding's coat, working it carefully over the handcuffs. Harding seemed to be under the impression that Longarm was going to do something about his broken collarbone. He said, "It's about time."

Longarm took off the vest the man was wearing, then undid the tie and stripped that off. The shirt followed and then the undershirt. The undershirt had to come over his head so Longarm didn't bother. He just ripped it off.

Harding was looking both annoyed and uncertain as he stood there, bare from the waist up. He said, "Here! What are you about?"

Longarm casually slapped him bare-handed across the mouth. A trickle of blood came out the corner of one of Harding's bruised lips. Longarm said, "I told you to keep quiet. Open that yap again and I'm going to break your nose. I hear tell you pride yourself on being a treat for the ladies to see. If you make any more noise, your own mother won't want to look at you, if you ever had one."

166

Now that he had stripped Harding bare, Longarm started to pull his hands behind his back again to complete the manacling but Harding protested, whispering, afraid to make any noise. He pleaded with Longarm, "Please. Please, Marshal. Handcuff me in front. It's killing my broken collarbone."

Longarm thought a moment, looking at the man. He said, "All right, but if you cause any trouble, it'll go that much worse for you."

Harding said, "I swear, Marshal. I won't be any trouble. Just please don't handcuff me behind my back."

Longarm shrugged and then handcuffed his wrists together in front of him. He stepped back. He said, "I'm going into the room next door. If you even move out of your tracks, I am going to come in here and have you for breakfast. Do you understand me? The door to the hall there is locked; you can't get out of it. This room is on the second story, and you can't get out of one of those windows. You can't get away from me and you're only going to agitate me if you try. Understand?"

Harding nodded mutely.

Longarm gave him one more look and then slipped quietly into the next room where Sarah was asleep. For a second, he looked down at her. She looked very little-girlish, relaxed with her hair arranged. A far cry from the whipped, frightened creature he had met not much more than a week previous. He leaned down and put his lips on hers, kissing her quietly until her eyes fluttered open. He was kissing her not only because he wanted to but also to keep her from yelling out. When he saw that she was awake, he pulled back and put his fingers to his lips.

He said, whispering to her, "I've got a surprise for you. It's going to scare you a little bit at first, but I think you're going to enjoy it."

167

She pulled herself up on one elbow. She asked, "What time is it?"

"I don't know. Probably about four o'clock in the morning."

"What kind of surprise can you have at four o'clock in the morning?" she asked.

"You just get up, get dressed, and turn the lamp up. You've got a good heavy robe, don't you?"

She nodded. He said, "Well, put that on. I don't want you showing too much."

She wrinkled her brow. "What kind of a surprise is it?"

He said, "It wouldn't be a surprise if I told you, now would it?"

She shook her head. She said, "You are the most amazing man."

"Hurry up and get dressed and call me when you're ready. Just call me—don't come to the door. I'll bring the surprise through the door."

Sarah threw the covers back and put her feet over the edge of the bed as he stood up. She said, "Well, you certainly have me curious."

"It's probably the last thing in the world that you ever expected to be surprised with." He turned around and walked back into his room. Harding was standing in exactly the same spot that Longarm had left him in. Longarm didn't think he had suddenly become obedient or any less defiant. He knew that the man had plenty of fight left in him, which was as he had hoped. Longarm wanted to watch it drain away under the hands of someone he himself had tortured and almost ruined.

Five minutes passed before Longarm heard the summons from the next room. He took Harding by the arm and turned him toward the connecting door. He was carrying the hard india rubber cane in his right hand. Harding asked, "Was that a woman's voice?"

"Not to you it ain't," Longarm said.

Harding said, "What's that supposed to mean?"

"You'll see."

They got to the doorway of the well-lit room and Longarm put his hand in the middle of Harding's back and shoved him forward. He heard a frightened shriek.

Chapter 12

He hustled around Harding, hurrying to reassure Sarah. She was dressed in a heavy quilted robe, but she was backed up against the end of her bed, her hands covering her face, her eyes fright-filled. Longarm went over to her. He said, "No, no, no, honey. You don't have to fear him anymore. He's yours now. The shoe's on the other foot."

She said in a trembling voice, "My God, it's Richard."

Harding walked a few steps into the room and asked, "What's she doing here?" He said it viciously, tearing off each word.

Longarm reached him in two steps, grabbed him by the arms, turned him and slammed him face forward toward the wall. He said, "Get over there and stay there and don't open that damned mouth again or I'll let some air into you."

Then he turned back to Sarah. He said, "Here's the man who tried to ruin your life. Here's the man who turned you into a hostage wife. Now, I'm going to give you the chance to give him some back." He held out the india rubber cane. "Have at him."

She looked at the cane and then she looked up at Longarm. She said slowly, shaking her head, "I couldn't. I couldn't."

Longarm said, "Hell, Sarah. He beat the living daylights out of you. What do you mean you can't? Of course you can."

Sarah shook her head. Her hands were down at her sides now but there was still horror and fear in her eyes. She said, "Oh, I couldn't. I couldn't."

From across the room, Harding laughed. "What's the matter, Longarm? Surprised? When I train them, I train them good."

"Listen to that! The damned fool is still shaming you. Take this cane and stripe his back good."

Sarah started, walking toward the front of the room where the little table stood with the water pitcher and the glasses on it. She poured herself a small glass of water and gulped it down. Longarm's bottle of whiskey was standing there. She said, "Can I have a drink?"

"Yes, by all means. Have a big one and then go beat the hell out of that son of a bitch," Longarm said.

She poured a tiny amount of whiskey in her glass and then added three times as much water. She drained it in one swallow and, after a moment, seemed to look calmer. She looked up at Longarm. She said, "I know you think you're doing me good, but it's not. I'm not that kind of person, Custis."

Longarm said, "All right, you can't hit him. That's fine. But I've seen the scars on your back and your breasts where he burnt you with a cigar." He fumbled in his pocket and got out a cigarillo and struck a match with the thick nail of his thumb, lit it and got it drawing good. He said, "Now there. Go plant a few of those burns on his back."

171

She looked at the glowing cigarillo and then she looked back up into Longarm's face. She said, "I can't do it, Custis. I can't do it."

Longarm said, "You have to hate that son of a bitch like nobody else in the world. Here's your chance to get back at him. Think of all the things he did to you. I saw you when you were whipped down like a dog."

"It doesn't matter," she said. "I can't be like him."

Longarm had his back to Harding. He heard the man laugh cruelly.

Harding said, "Ain't working out like you'd planned, is it, Longarm? I could have told you that. Little Miss Sarah ain't got the backbone of a turnip. She's too sweet, she's too nice. I had a lot of fun, playing with her. She never did learn how to fuck though, Longarm. I don't guess you found that out being the gentleman that you are. She didn't know how."

Longarm said savagely, "Shut your damn mouth, Harding." He looked back around at Sarah. She had blushed scarlet. He said, "Doesn't that make you want to give him a little of what he gave you? Doesn't that make you want to help him out? Give him a thrill or two?"

Sarah just shook her head again. "I couldn't, Custis. I couldn't hurt someone just to be hurting them. I don't ever want to be like him. I know that I should, but I can't."

Longarm was frustrated and nettled. He said, "Damn it, Sarah. I went to considerable trouble to bring this son of a bitch up here to let you get yours back at him and now you're telling me no. That don't make a lick of sense. If he'd done to me what he done to you, I'd take him outside and bury him up to his nose and leave him there for about a month."

She said, "I know you're trying to help me and you are doing this for my own good. But I can't do it."

"You'll end up spending your hate on him the rest of your life. Get it out right now. Get it out, take it out on him."

"I don't even really hate him."

Longarm looked up at the ceiling and sighed. He said, "That don't make no sense, Sarah. Here, take this cigarillo and go over there and put a hole in his back." He was holding the cigarillo out toward her, motioning for her to take it from him.

Suddenly, Sarah let out a scream and shoved him. For an instant, he didn't realize what had happened. She had shoved him hard enough so that he stumbled backward. As he stumbled, there was the sudden roar of a gunshot. Instinctively, Longarm's hand whipped down to his own revolver. He was falling backward, turning to his left and drawing at the same time. As he came around, he saw Harding at the end of the room. He had found the gun that had belonged to Chulo that Longarm had left on the table near the window. He had it thrust out in front of him in both hands. He was cocking it for another shot as Longarm cleared leather with his revolver. He hit the floor on his left side, his right arm going straight out. He thumbed the hammer back on the .44-caliber pistol, and aiming straight at the center of Harding's chest, he fired an instant before Harding could get off a second shot. The impact of the bullet knocked Harding backward into the window shade. Longarm could vaguely hear glass breaking. He thumbed the hammer again and fired as Harding pitched forward. The second slug caught him high in the shoulder, knocking him back against the sill of the window. Harding slowly rolled forward and then was still.

Through the haze and the noise, Longarm looked up from the floor, searching for Sarah. The last time he'd seen her, she'd been standing by the little wash table. He raised up and saw her lying on the floor. He dropped his gun and hurried to her as quickly as he could. Her robe was light blue and he looked carefully for the dreaded crimson stain. There was none. He began rapidly to unbutton the robe. She was white, pale. Her eyes were closed. He got the robe unbuttoned all the way down the front and opened it up. Then he saw the blood. It was on her upper arm. Because she was still wearing her nightgown, he couldn't tell if the bullet had broken bone or not. He took her nightgown by the neck and ripped it down the left side. To his relief, he could see that the bullet had hit her shoulder, tearing through the soft flesh, but it had obviously missed the bone. The impact had knocked her down and the pain and the fright had made her faint.

Longarm cursed himself for being such a damned fool as to have turned his back on a man like Harding, but then he'd been so cocky, so confident that he had the situation in hand that he had forgotten all about the gun. If Sarah hadn't seen Harding aim the gun and shoved him aside, it would have been he, Longarm, who would have taken the bullet squarely in the back. He caressed Sarah's hair for just a second before getting to his feet. She needed a doctor. She wasn't losing much blood, but she was losing some. He was about to rise when there came a sudden knocking on the door and a babble of voices.

He yelled, "Get a doctor! Now! Get a doctor!"

While he waited for the doctor, he got up and walked over and looked down at Richard Harding. The man had caused trouble and violence and evil for the last time. Longarm was furious that he had gotten off so lightly, with just a bullet. He couldn't help himself. He drew back his leg and kicked Harding in the ribs as hard as he could, knowing the man was far past feeling anything. Somehow, though, it made him feel better. Then he quickly went back to Sarah's side. She was beginning to stir and moan. He smoothed her hair and talked softly to her, waiting for the doctor to come.

Chapter 13

It took the better part of a week for Longarm to get the whole business wound up and all the loose ends tied down. By the end of that time, he felt he was about as sick of Laredo and its environs as any place he had ever been. It seemed like a year ago since he'd taken the train to Mexico City to bring Earl Combs back. It seemed like a month since he'd walked Richard Harding in to face his wife. He guessed Sarah's attitude toward revenge made her a better person than he was. It still made him angry that Richard Harding had gotten out so easy with a bullet. Longarm would have much preferred for him to have spent the rest of his life breaking rocks in a federal prison in Arizona.

The biggest chore of all had been the examiners and the investigators from the federal banking system who had come down at his signal that the matter was finally ending. He had gotten the key to the safety-deposit box from Earl Combs and had gone himself and made certain that the money was in box 509 before he telegraphed the proper authorities. It had been there, although it was short ten thousand dollars. Combs at first refused to admit that he had taken the money, citing some imaginary partner. But they both knew better, and in the end, Combs admitted that he had taken the money to live on until the trail had cooled and he could come back for the rest of the money some distant day in the future. Longarm had been surprised that he had left the money in Laredo, but Combs had given him an astonished look. He said, "You certainly didn't think I was going to take that amount of cash outside of the United States, did you?"

Longarm stared at him and nodded. He said, "No, I reckon not."

Combs said, "Why, do you have any idea how many thieves there are in Mexico? How many highwaymen? How many robbers?"

Longarm had smiled and said, "No, but I do know there is one less now that you're in jail on this side of the river."

About five investigators and examiners had descended on him. When they counted the money, they'd given him suspicious looks and asked what did he reckon went with that extra ten thousand dollars. Longarm explained over and over again about the entire matter. He reckoned, in total, he told the story from when he picked up Combs to when he killed Richard Harding over half a dozen times. Sarah, who was one of the main witnesses, was spared most of the questioning because of her wound.

It had turned out that Billy Vail's telegram had not quite worked. It had taken another telegram from the chief marshal to a couple of senators who were friends of his to force the Treasury officials into turning Combs over to Federal Judge Richard Harding. The most curious part of the matter to Longarm was the investigators' and examiners' apparent disbelief that Judge Harding had been up to any kind of criminal activity. It was only after they had gone through his court docket, interviewed his court clerks, and interviewed a number of the citizens around Laredo that they found out the extent of his deviousness and chicanery and plain out-and-out criminality. That he had kept his wife a virtual hostage had no significance to the bank examiners and investigators. They were more concerned with ledgers and figures and cash amounts than what had happened to a twenty-seven-year-old and her good heart and blithe spirit.

The Treasury bunch, as Longarm had begun to call them in his mind, had finally departed, taking the money and Earl Combs with them. Longarm had seen Combs off at the train. He hoped he never saw the man and a train at the same time again so long as he lived. Combs was still in some pain. The burns on his feet forced him to wear slippers and he had .splints on three fingers as well as severe burns on one hand. Longarm had tried to cheer him up by saying, "Well, Earl, at least they won't hand you a sledgehammer, not right off anyway. Look on the bright side of it." Combs gave him a sour look and boarded the northbound train.

Then there had been Sarah to get straightened out. Her wound had shocked her more than it had hurt her. It had gone through the fleshy part of her shoulder and she had bled quite a bit, but in the end it was a trivial matter. The doctor had made her stay in bed for three days, and her arm was not to be used so that the wound would heal faster. She had been relieved that it was all over, but like a man suddenly let out of jail after a long term, the free world looked frightening and unreal to her. She asked Longarm, "What will I do? I don't know anything to do. I have no family left and I'm not trained for anything. Perhaps I can get a job at the hotel."

Longarm laughed. He had already arranged matters. During a break with the bank people, he'd paid a visit to Richard Harding's lawyer, who turned out surprisingly enough to be an honest man. Harding had not made a will and Sarah, being his legal spouse, was entitled to inherit everything he owned. Longarm and the lawyer had paid a call on the attractive young woman who was presenting herself as the second Mrs. Harding. She was a showgirl from New Orleans and she took the news in good humor. She'd said, "Yeah, I guess it was too good to last. It was really nice living with a rich man and not having to go to bed with him. That part I liked. It's been a good vacation, but I guess I'm about ready to go back to work anyway."

Within three days, she had moved out, bag and baggage, and was never seen again.

While investigating Harding's assets, Longarm discovered he had $21,000 in cash at the bank, another $20,000 in municipal bonds as well as the deed to the big house in town that was completely paid for and which Longarm thought would fetch a considerable sum. He also owned in full the hacienda in Mexico and the cabin. Sarah was going to be well provided for.

He let her worry just for his own amusement for about half a day. Then when she was able to be up and around, he'd hired a carriage from the livery stable and driven her out to the house she had once occupied for a short time as the wife of Richard Harding. It had frightened her, going to the house, and it took quite a bit of persuasion on his part to get her out of the carriage and up the walkway and onto the porch. But there she balked. She said, "There'll be someone in there. That woman is in there. We can't go in."

At that point, faced with her absolute reluctance, he'd had to tell her that the house belonged to her and that the woman was gone, that she was now mistress of the place.

They'd gone in and he'd stood and watched as she ghosted through the big house, seeing it, he supposed, for the first time with completely new eyes. She wandered around for the better part of two hours. When she finally came back to Longarm, she said sadly, "It's a wonderful house but it has a bad feel about it. It feels like he's still here. I don't want to live here."

Longarm shrugged. He said, "Me and the lawyer done figured that much. He's got a buyer already lined up who will give you forty thousand dollars for the place."

Her eyes got big and her lips parted slightly. She said, "Forty thousand dollars! That's a fortune."

Little by little, he had let her find out about the rest of her assets. When he finished, he said, "My lady, you're a very rich woman. Some handsome young man is going to come along and sweep you off your feet and you're going to wonder if it's you or the money. Let me tell you right now, it'll be you."

She'd looked at him and said, "Do you ever think about marrying, Custis?"

He shook his head and smiled. "It ain't good policy to marry U.S. deputy marshals. It's not the kind of work that makes for a happy home life. It doesn't make for a good marriage if the husband is always gone or getting shot at."

She smiled at him again. "I knew you were going to say that but I couldn't help but ask." She reached up and touched his cheek. "You do know that you are very special to me. Not just because you saved my life, not just because you gained me my freedom. I learned a lot from you."

He leaned down and kissed her gently on the lips. "You are very special to me also, Sarah, and I've learned a lot from you. I know now that everything in life doesn't have to be hard and rough and hurtful. You're quite a lady."

She had been unsure of her plans, but she did know that she was going to leave Laredo and the border country.

Longarm said, "I think that's a good idea. This ain't no

place for a gentle woman. This place is bad. If you stay here long enough, you go bad."

She looked up at him. "Do you think that's what happened to Richard?"

He shook his head. He said, "No, I think Richard Harding just brought more evil to an already bad place, like so many others who have come here. No, the border didn't corrupt Richard Harding. He was meant for this strip of ground."

She had thought perhaps with the money she now had that she would go back to Kentucky. Maybe even live in the town she had grown up in.

Longarm said, "At least that way you will meet the kind of man you should have."

Even with her shoulder to be careful of, they'd still managed to have three wonderful nights together. It was the kind of sex that Longarm had almost forgotten about. She was so unknowledgeable, so fresh, so new, so virginlike. It was a pleasure for him to lead her slowly through the erotic paths of passion and ecstasy and climax. With his lips and his tongue and his penis and his fingertips, he had taught her about her body, slowly drawing her out until she would almost quiver with the power of her excitement. He had stood her naked in front of a full-length mirror and showed her what a beautiful woman she was, showed her how perfectly shaped her full breasts were with their big nipples, showed her on the bed how perfectly they fit together. Now, it took him only a few minutes to bring her to a warm, moist readiness, ready to receive him as he thrust into her. It had been three nights he didn't suppose he would ever forget. Neither would he forget the sight of her body in his mind's eye. She was as close to being the perfect woman as he guessed he had ever seen. He knew part of that was because when he'd first seen her, she'd looked so dowdy and lumpy in the blanket-material robe with her tangled and tousled hair. To have such a butterfly emerge from an ugly cocoon had something to do with it, he was sure. But yet, simply lying in bed and looking at her as she stood before him with her lips slightly parted and her big gray-blue eyes and her light brown wavy hair curving down around her shoulders, he had to admire her small waist, the slight mound of her stomach, her straight, shapely legs joining in the downy thatch of light brown silken hair. No, she was truly one of the most perfect women he had ever met, and it was with more than a trace of sadness that he had told her good-bye when he left the hotel. She had wanted to come with him to the train to see him off but he wouldn't have it. He had explained to her in the room that he wanted to tell her good-bye properly and leave with that kind of good-bye as a memory, not some hurried kiss among a flock of strangers beside a train hissing steam.

So they had parted that way, and now he sat in the same saloon and at the same table he'd occupied on that disastrous day some two weeks past when Mr. Jenkins had begun casting glances his way. He hadn't planned it as a man would who had started a job and hadn't completed it and was determined to come back to finish. He had not said to himself, "I'm going to go into that saloon, sit down and have a drink, and catch the train this time. This time, I'm not going to Mexico on some wild-goose chase."

No, it had been much simpler than that. The train had been reported late and he thought it would be better to be sitting drinking whiskey while he waited, than hanging around a train depot.

Still he did find it funny. He was not much looking forward to getting home to Denver, in spite of the lady dressmaker he was very fond of who lived there, the one who lived in the same boarding house and liked to be taken unawares. She liked to play dress up and then dress down. Longarm was a broad-minded man. If what he was after was at the end of it, he was quite willing to wind through a rabbit warren as cheerfully as the next man. What he mainly dreaded about getting back to Denver was trying to explain this whole mess to Billy Vail and to write the report and, after that, to make out his expense voucher. That was going to be some piece of business. He'd turned his horse back in to the horse trader he'd bought him from and got one hundred seventy-five dollars in return. He figured he could just write that twenty-five dollars off. Billy Vail would say, "Twenty-five dollars to rent a horse for a week? Are you crazy? Do you think the United States government is made out of money?" And of course, there'd been no hope of shipping the horse back to Denver even though it was, technically, government property. Billy would have thrown a fit over that.

Longarm sighed and poured some more whiskey in his glass. It was coming up time to go back over to the depot. He sipped slowly at the whiskey, which may have been the best Laredo had to offer but was nowhere near as good as his Maryland whiskey that he was now out of until he got home. He dreaded the trip, he dreaded the paperwork, he dreaded the kidding he was going to get about being taken hostage by a federal judge. He shook his head slowly to himself. He knew without even thinking hard about it that this was one that he was probably never going to hear the end of. Taken hostage? Him? Longarm? Wrapped up and tied with a red ribbon and delivered to a hacienda in Mexico? He wondered if there was any way he could lie his way out of it, but there didn't seem to be any.

The saloon was almost as deserted as it had been the day he had been in there with Mr. Jenkins. He suddenly noticed a man standing at the bar, looking at him over his shoulder. The man was dressed in ordinary business clothes. He could have been a merchant, he could have been a drummer, he could have been a bank clerk. Longarm didn't care what he was. The instant he saw the man looking at him, he threw down the last of his whiskey in his glass, picked up his valise, and walked straight out of the saloon as fast as he could go, heading for the depot. This was one train he wasn't going to miss.

If you enjoyed this book, subscribe now and get...

TWO FREE

A $7.00 VALUE–

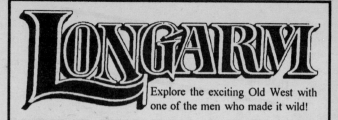